3
THE DRAGON CROWN SERIES

Court of Dragons and Ashes

G. BAILEY

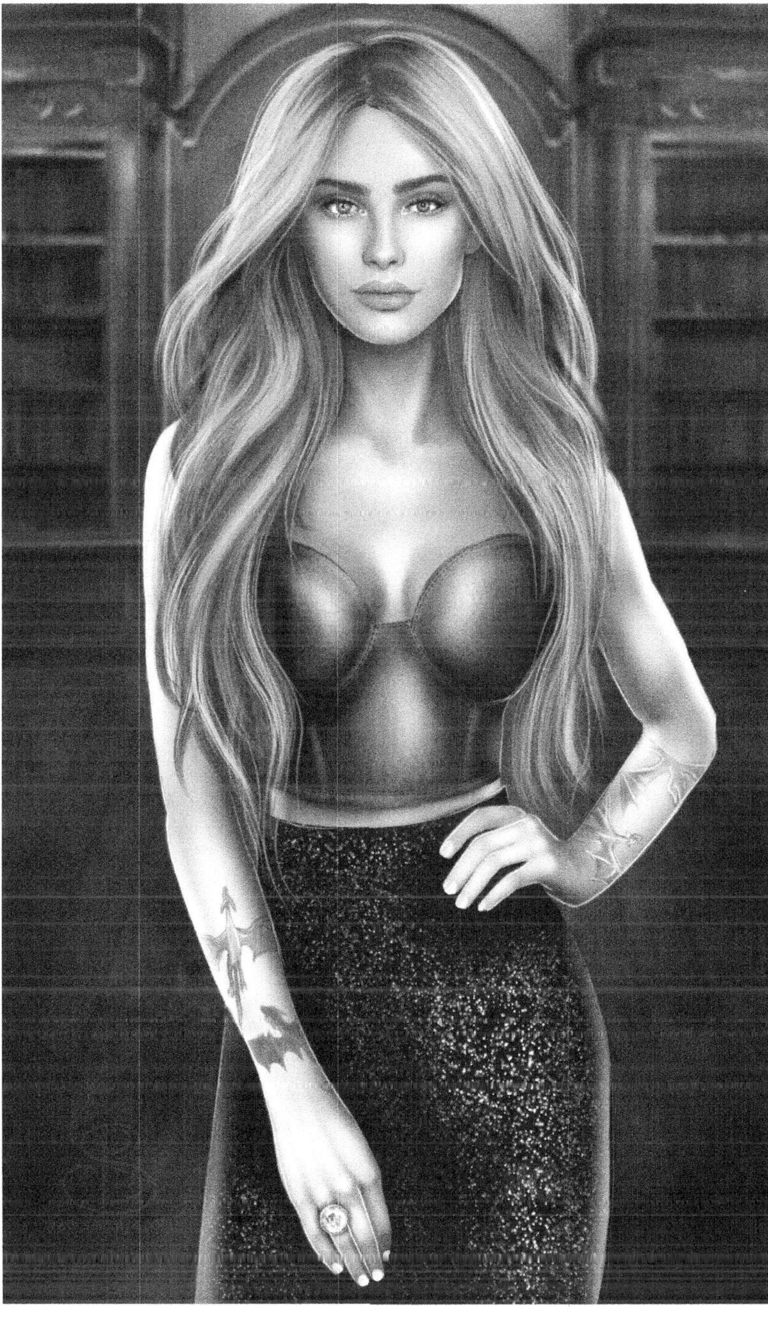

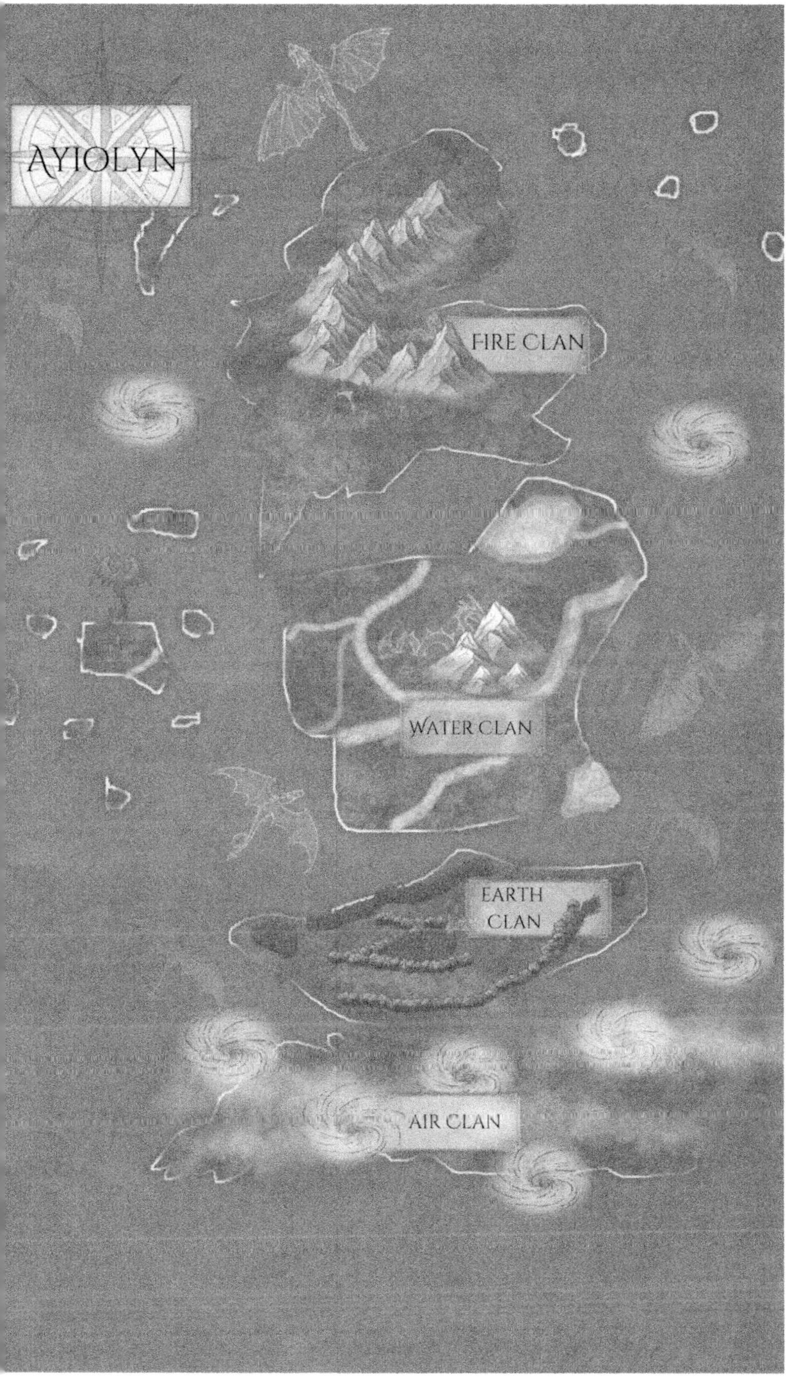
AYIOLYN
FIRE CLAN
WATER CLAN
EARTH
CLAN
AIR CLAN

COURT OF DRAGONS AND ASHES
THE DRAGON CROWN SERIES
BOOK THREE

G. BAILEY

CONTENTS

Description	xi
Prologue	1
Chapter 1	15
Chapter 2	34
Chapter 3	45
Chapter 4	56
Chapter 5	76
Chapter 6	93
Chapter 7	104
Chapter 8	122
Chapter 9	132
Chapter 10	149
Chapter 11	157
Chapter 12	180
Chapter 13	203
Chapter 14	218
Epilogue	233
Afterword	239
About the Author	241
Other Books by G. Bailey	243

Part I
BONUS READ OF HEIR OF MONSTERS

Bonus read of Heir of Monsters	247
1. Bonus read of Heir of Monsters	251
2. Bonus read of Heir of Monsters	276
The Missing Wolf	285
The Missing Wolf	293

Court of Dragons and Ashes
All Rights Reserved. 2024.

This is a work of fiction. Names, characters, places, and incidents either are the products of the author's imagination or are used fictitiously. Any resemblance to actual persons, living or dead, businesses, companies, events, or locales is entirely coincidental and formed by this author's imagination. No part of this book may be reproduced or used in any manner without the express written permission of the publisher except for the use of brief quotations in a book review.
Edited by Polished Perfection

Cover by MiblArt
Artwork by Samaiya Art.
Trigger Warning: Mentions/memories of near SA. Feel free to email at gbaileyauthor@gmail.com for more information, as your mental health matters.

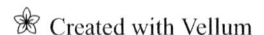

❊ Created with Vellum

DESCRIPTION

The goddess of love has designed a deadly trial, and if I don't win…I will lose my dragon kings.

In the court of Water, a monster lurks.
In the court of Fire, flames burn away any lies.
In the court of Earth, touch is key.
In the court of Air, try to breathe.

Aphrodite has my dragon kings under her spell, and to save them, I have to win four trials, one in each court. Ares may not be able to kill me, but the courts are dangerous with him in charge, and he isn't going to let me win easily. With enemies within the courts, and outside them too, I need allies to survive this.

I was born of shadows, royalty, and hope.
When I call, Ayiolyn will rise.

This is a full-length enemies to lovers fantasy romance with dragon shifters, a badass heroine, and possessive alpha males. Perfect for fans of spicy fantasy whychoose? romance. This is book three of the Dragon Crown series; the books must be read in order.

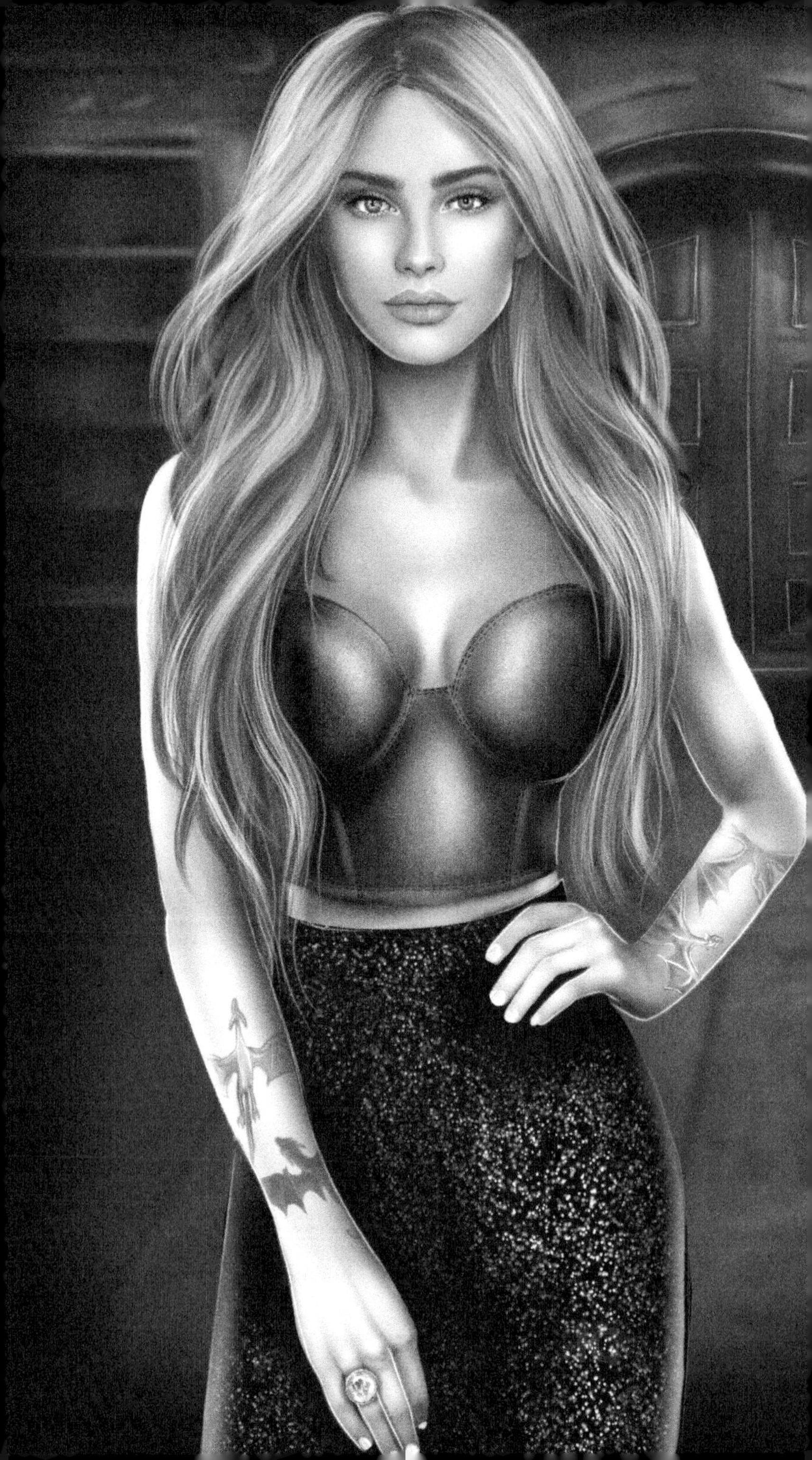

PROLOGUE

FALKEN ILROTH, KING OF THE SPIRIT COURT

My life has been marked by the decisions I've made. To be a king. To love my mate and wife. To have a child. Life isn't usually marked by dreams…but this is no ordinary dream, and I know it will haunt me for years to come.

There have been several dreams in my life that I knew were filled with magic, filled with a warning that must be listened to. When I was ten years old, I dreamt of the most beautiful young woman I'd ever seen in my life. She had long black hair, bright blue eyes, and she was stunning. She was standing on a stone pier, watching out over a stormy sea, in a world that was not one that I'd grown up in. A mortal world. I was aware of Earth, and I had always been called to it, never understanding why. I knew, without an inch of doubt in my mind, that I had to find this woman in my lifetime. I had to meet her, because she would be mine.

Of course, I was only a child, so when I woke up, fitfully talking about this strange woman that I'd seen, my parents thought I was completely insane and had lost my mind. But years later, I met her on that exact pier. The same thing happened in the dream, but I was in the shadow, watching her from a distance. This time, I was there when she turned around and looked at me with the same shock, awe, and instant attraction I felt. I knew she was my mate. I knew without any doubt in my heart that this woman was the love of my life and that there would be no one before or after her that would make me feel this way.

Naturally, she was stubborn and more powerful than I could've possibly imagined. She was the daughter of a goddess, and her powers met my own, perfectly matched. I convinced her to come to my world, to my castle, to be my queen. It came with a cost. She didn't want to leave Earth, a world her mother was trapped in. But she loved me, and together we paid any price for our love.

But this current dream, it doesn't fill me with

hope. It fills me with dread, with a dread that turns my stomach into a pit of ashes. I look across my lands from the top of my castle, tasting the death and despair thick in the air. The land around the castle—filled with houses, temples, structures, and beauty—is burning. Everything's being destroyed, blown up with magic, and dragons are falling from the skies.

I'm not alone. A cloaked enemy, who I can barely see, stands before me. He holds a staff that calls to me. "Your time is over, King. The Spirit Court has fallen. Your wife, your daughter, they are both dead, as will your people soon be. There'll be no one here to remember the Spirit Court, and when I'm done, every court will fall to me. I will be the only ruler left."

I gasp as this man rips me apart with magic until only my soul is there to watch as my world is completely destroyed by a god who will never stop. Words fill my mind, powerful and old, full of warning. "A princess of spirit, bound to each element, will be born to the night, promised with hope. In her blood lies the secrets of Ayiolyn, and she needs only call. In the sacred elements, bonds will be forged. She will find her destined mates in the courts of shadow, fire, water, air, and earth."

Waking up in my room, I listen only to my heart racing as sweat pours down my brow. My shadows flood the room, coming to protect me, but I send them away. Even they are no comfort now. I need my queen. I pat the empty space next to me and frown. "She is fine, your majesty."

I turn, facing the matron, who is standing over the end of my bed. "What are you doing in here?" The matron never comes into our rooms. "Where's my wife?"

"She's in labour, my king. Congratulations." The matron bows her head. Joy fills my senses, and even the darkness seems to lighten. "It's only the start, and the queen didn't want to wake you. She's gone to walk round the castle with her friends. She sent me to inform you that you should be ringing the castle bells, making the court aware that the new prince or princess will be here soon. It is your honour to do so, after all."

The bells haven't rung since I was born. "I must see her…" I stop. I can't tell her about this dream, not now, not when she needs to concentrate on labouring our child. I sit up, frowning.

The matron is too smart. I've always known that about her. "You had a dream?" She pauses. "No, a dream of the future, and it has frightened you."

Lifting my head, I look at the matron. She isn't mortal, dragon, goddess, or anything I can label, and for a time, I wanted to know what she is and why she stays here. I remember my father telling me she had been there since he was a boy, and his grandfather talked about the matron to him once, suggesting she has lived a very long time. She is a being who's lived in this castle longer than I could know, full of secrets that no one possibly could guess. But she's loyal to the castle, first and foremost, and she's loyal to my family.

I don't even know how old she is. She looks like a harmless old lady, aged and withered. But I've seen her fight, moving quicker than any wind could blow. There are a lot of secrets about her, and I doubt she is here on a whim. My queen could have sent anyone with the news. She turns from me, looking out past the balcony. "I was awoken by the magic haunting you, calling to me like a song. I feel you must tell me about your dreams, my king, as they might speak to my own foretellings of the future."

"It was less a dream than a nightmare," I answer. I've spent my entire life being wary around people in this court, as all kings have enemies. Our court, we have plenty. But I trust her with my life. So did my father and his father before him.

"A prophecy, a forecasting of what's to come," she guesses, her voice like ice.

"I've had them since I was a child." My answer lingers between us as I decide to trust her with this. I cannot tell my queen right at this moment, but I will. When she is stronger, when our child is here and safe. I climb out of the bed, walking over to the window where there's a small table. I pour myself a glass of wine and down it, wincing at the bitter taste, before I tell the matron what the dream was about.

Afterwards, silence rings between us, thick and heavy. The matron walks over to my side, watching out across the kingdom. It won't be long until the sun rises, flooding the dark kingdom with light, but with the way I feel, I almost sense the morning will never come. The sun will never rise the same way, not now I know death is on its way for me. "I have had dreams like this, too. The fall of the Spirit Court. I do not see this enemy's true face, as you put him. Just a danger, coming for us all."

"I have to stop it," I bite, clutching the glass tightly in my hand. "My child is being born soon, and they cannot come into a world where that is the future."

"The future can be changed; all dreams can be," she remarks. "I highly doubt the two things are not coincidental."

"The monster said that he killed my daughter. I am to have a daughter," I whisper. Pride fills my chest and longing. We've wanted a child since the early days of our relationship, and she was our miracle, made on our mating day. Our princess.

"I know of magic so dangerous and powerful that your grandfather forbade it," the matron begins.

I know of this magic. My father warned me of it so I might warn the future generations. Death magic. My parents are gone from this world. They cast themselves into shadows years ago when I was only a teenager. I never knew why they decided to leave. Maybe they were done with life. They were always different from how I am. They were colder, empty. The Spirit Court did not thrive under their ruling. My mother always was looking for something else. Looking for a life outside of this castle. My father only cared about the magic that lay deep within the shadows.

"To protect your people, you will need this magic. You will need to pull all the magic of every ancestor before you out of the shadows with death magic, through your body and soul."

My mouth goes dry. To use that magic…it would curse my soul. Destroy it. I would never find my mate or child in the afterlife; I would be lost. Forever.

"You were born a king, and it is your choice, but you have seen what happens if you do nothing. Save them. The children. The babies. The women. The men. Give them a chance to live, as many as you can. Some will stay to fight, but—"

"Are you insane? That kind of magic…" I whisper, but I can't finish the sentence, as the nightmare haunts me. So many dead, so many lost. Is the price of my own life worth all of theirs if I'm destined to die either way?

"It looks like you are going to lead yourself to death either way and take your court, wife, and child with you."

I pause at that. She's right, of course. Death is what my dreams showed me, and my dreams have always come true. Every single one. But this one felt different, more powerful, more of a warning than I've ever had before. There is much to be said about a king who dies protecting everyone. I swore to protect my people when I took my crown, promised to be a better ruler than my parents.

"When your child grows, she will need her people. She will need an army to fight for her, and she will have nothing if this court falls and is destroyed. You know who he is."

Tears fill my eyes. "So will you." Though, we do not speak his name, not here, not in my home. I barely even want to think of his name. Time will reveal him to her, to every court. "But if that evil is returning to us, I must inform the other kings, call them to fight."

"You can do that. At the end. I always foresee the courts being united, but I do not think it's your generation that will unite them," she answers, her eyes glazed over with magic.

"My daughter?" I ask, desperate to know she will have a future. Dying for her…I will do it. I will save my people, my wife and child. The Spirit Court must live on, even if there is nothing of me left. We have time, I hope we do. My dream will not come true yet, but when it is time…

The door's knocked once and we both turn. "Come in!"

A young boy toddles in. The matron's four-year-old ward. No one knows where he and his baby sister came from, but this young little boy isn't her son. She just turned up with him as a baby, claimed that he was family to her, and he must be brought up in the castle. His sister turned up a few months ago and is sleeping in the nursery, another mystery. We asked Matron if any more were planning on turning up, but she claimed no, that these two are the last. My wife loves him, always buying him gifts, and he has a room a few down from our own.

I sense great untouched magic within his soul, and the dark shadows crawl out of the corners to see the child. To communicate with him. I push them away, not wanting them to scare the child. They can wait until he is older.

"Terrin," the matron softly speaks, and the boy grins, missing one little tooth he lost when he climbed the castle and fell off, despite all our warnings not to climb alone. His black hair is short, his eyes bright with childhood innocence. "Thank you for coming, my little boy. We have something to tell you about a prophecy."

I swing my head to the matron. "We can't tell this boy anything. This must be kept a secret."

"Agreed," the matron tells me. "But, my king, the prophecy you heard speaks of my ward." She cups the boy's face, who looks warily at me. "Terrin, these are words you must remember as you grow older and guide the army of the Spirit Court."

"This boy cannot be left to lead," I say to the matron.

"He can because he will be the mate of your daughter. Shadow, as foretold, is he," the matron informs me, and I look at the boy. It's hard to imagine a future where he will be at the side of my daughter, who I have not even met. "He must remember the prophecy as he grows. He must fly the dragons to the west, where I believe they will be able to hide. One day, he will be at your daughter's side, and he should come with the knowledge of how to help her. I foresee that I will not be able to help, or even recognise your daughter when the time comes. You tell him the prophecy, my king."

"Whose child is he?" I demand, well aware the boy is watching, taking everything in.

Matron smiles at him. "He was born within shadows, created in darkness just like me, and that is all the truth I can tell you. The answer is for him to find when he is older, when he comes asking, hopefully with his princess at his side."

I look at the boy who will be the mate of my unborn daughter, and nod. I kneel down at his level, something a king should not do. He is family, and I will protect him as best I can. "I'm going to transform you into a dragon to protect you in the years to come, and I need you to remember something for me. A story, a very important story." He bows his head. Even this young, he is older than his time. "I'm going to tell you a prophecy about a baby who's not even born yet, and then, one day in the future, please save my daughter."

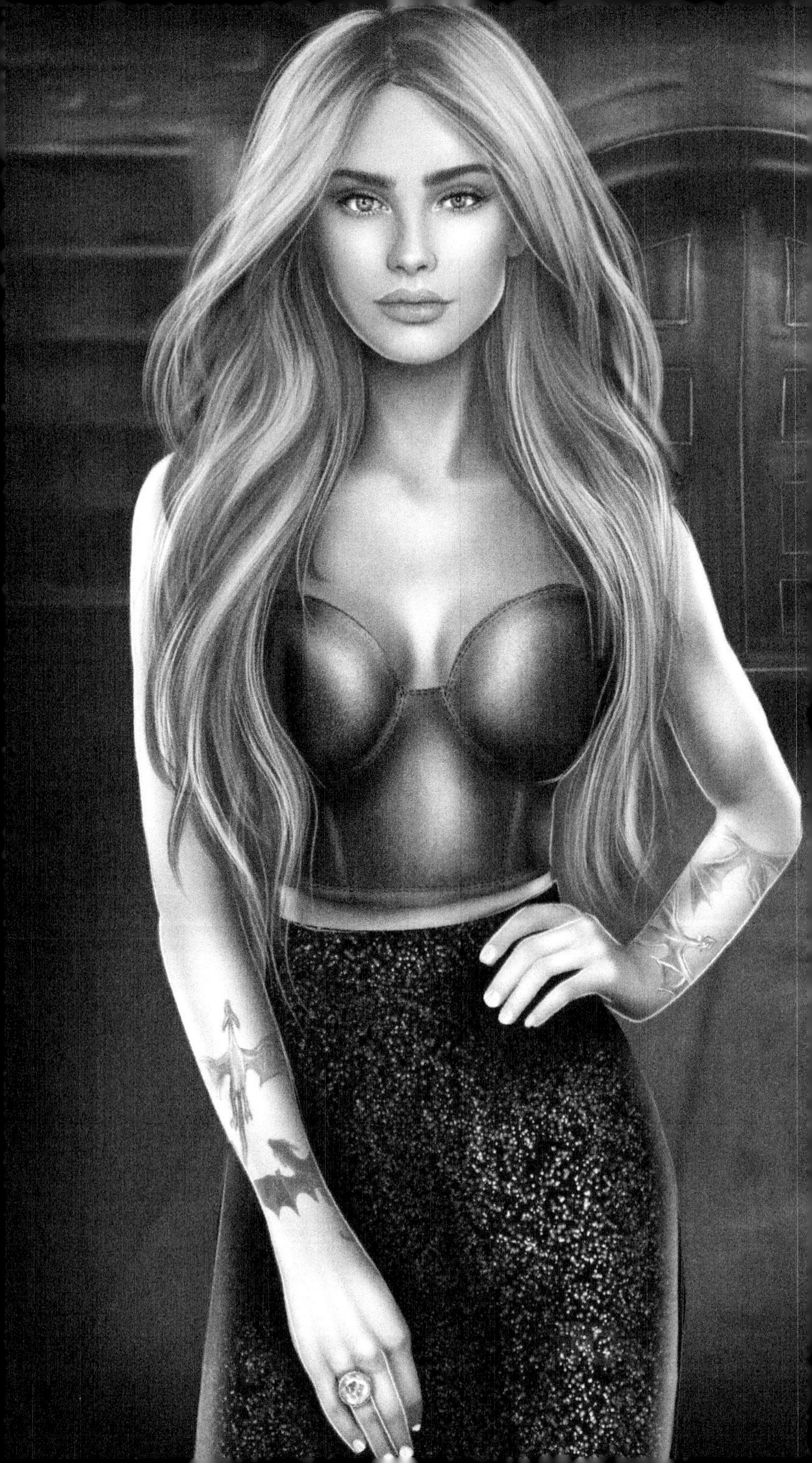

CHAPTER 1

Making the choice to trust a backstabbing liar is one of the worst decisions I could knowingly make. Or at least, that's what Hope keeps repeating to me, and I don't think she is wrong. Arty watches me from the living room, her locks of blonde hair covering her left cheek where it's bruised—and not from my attack earlier. My clothes are dry now, the truth is out, and I should feel more in control, but I don't. I feel like I'm spiralling into another world, another person, and there isn't anyone here to stop me from drowning, because the men I love decided to sacrifice themselves and abandon me.

My shoulders drop slightly. They didn't abandon me; I *know* that, but the bitter sting is something I'm not sure I can push aside. I chose to be with them, for us to face our battles together, and each one of them decided to leave me on Earth and take on an insane goddess on their own.

My grandmother's soft voice echoes. "Are you ready, Elle?"

Am I?

Turning to my grandmother, Hera, I can't help but be silenced by the memories that are still flooding back to me. Hera is my grandmother. I'm the granddaughter of a goddess, and I have powers, strong powers that have been honed by gods. I was never much good at the mind control aspect of my powers I inherited from her and my mother, but shadows? They breathed for me, and they still do.

My grandmother is the goddess of marriage, of family and rebirth...and she brought me up to be stronger than I feel right at this moment. My mum and dad brought me up to be a princess of the fifth court, with all the power of an heir of darkness and shadows...and I don't know what my mother is going to say when she sees me. That is, *if* she's really still alive.

Hope and Livia watch me from the kitchen door, both of them worried, but they haven't told anyone what happened to me. I close my eyes for a moment, a flashback smacking into my mind of him, and suddenly I can't breathe. I step away from them all, facing the back wall of the kitchen and sucking in a deep breath as the memory fades away. When it does, I notice it's silent and shadows flood the floor, like a carpet made of my magic. They don't touch my family or friends, who shouldn't need to fear the darkness. My father's lessons come back to me, how he took me to the pits of darkness in the base of the castle, of our home, and taught me their ways. "Elle?"

I let the shadows retreat and sink into the cracks in the tiles, waiting for my call. "I'm ready to leave. We should go into the garden."

My grandmother steps in front of me, cupping my face, her eyes softly glowing in the dim light of dawn as it casts a yellow haze through the windows. Even with light flooding the small room and glowing all around her, I can see nothing but the darkness in every corner, whispering to me, promising me revenge if I seek it. My father once warned me that spirit, the magic of darkness and shadow, is fed by our emotions. It reacts to them, breathes them, and right now I'm not in control. "You've grown stronger since you left, but there is a darkness, something you're not telling me, and it's hovering over your mind now."

"I need to get to them and see if Arty isn't lying about mum," I answer, stepping out of her grip. I can't talk to her about what happened, not yet. I reach again for Lysander, for Terrin and the small bonds I can feel with the others now, but nothing. I can't feel them.

Her troubled eyes stay with me as she opens a drawer in the kitchen side and pulls out a small magical box. The box looks like a normal flatware holder. I've passed it a dozen times, but with my memories back, I remember it. She hands it to me, and I place it on the counter. I wave my hand over the box, a gift from my uncle. Several locks click inside before the top slides open. Inside are two daggers, ancient and ornate, possessing their own magic and souls. Uncle Phobos taught me of the legends of these daggers, how they once were people who used too much magic and ended up transforming themselves into these weapons. One blade is black, the other white, and they are diamond encrusted except for the black leather hilts. I pull them out of the box and hide them in the shadows so I can get to them whenever I want.

Livia walks over, looking around like she can

see the daggers in the darkness. "I'm never going to get used to you using magic so easily." Jinks runs into the room, jumping right into Livia's arms. The white cat with glowing red eyes purrs innocently. "He's such a sweet cat."

My grandmother flashes me a grin for a second. We both know he isn't just a cat, and he isn't sweet at all. Livia would drop him in a second if she knew. I almost smile.

Hope steps forward. "We shouldn't waste any more time." She looks right into my eyes. "They will need us, now more than they ever have. I don't care if this is what they wanted for you. We all know you won't leave them there, right?"

"I'm furious with them for making a choice I didn't ask for or want, but I would never leave them to the fate they have woven to protect me." My statement lingers in the air. "I haven't met Aphrodite, but she has them. I wish they had told me about the deal."

Arty clears her throat. "I believe the deal was to be your mate, all four of them, before the time was up. I believe they wanted you to make the decision yourself, not feel forced."

I feel as uncomfortable as I can possibly get when everyone looks right at me, like I'm meant to have all of the answers and know everything to do now I remember. My grandmother watches me with interest. "Are you dating one of them? How could she expect you to mate all four kings when…" Her gaze drifts off. "Ah, fate has been interesting."

"They belong to her." Hope waves her hand at me when I can't answer. "All four of them, and they are fools for not being honest."

My grandmother's face creases. "In all my time, in all my immortal life, I have not met one person who isn't a fool in the name of love. It is not a sin, not a mistake, and they wished to protect you. I like these kings already."

"I want you to meet them," I softly reply.

She smiles brightly. "Then you best go back to your world and get them. You are a princess of the Spirit Court, granddaughter to the goddess Hera, and more powerful than anyone I've known. Never forget it, never let anyone try to steal your power and light." My heart races. It's almost like she knows what almost happened to me, what is haunting my every step. "Just come back alive. I've already lost nearly my entire family in that world. A world I can't even step in to help."

I can't promise her anything, but I nod once, and she kisses my cheek. Hope leans on the counter next to us. "Why is that? Why can't you go into Ayiolyn but Aphrodite and Ares are there? And trapped?"

My grandmother sighs. "Ares entered Ayiolyn first, pulling along Aphrodite after a few hundred years of destruction and pain. The people in Ayiolyn had their own magic, and they blocked anyone else after Aphrodite because they knew their world couldn't handle another god. They couldn't get rid of them, but they did their best to make sure no gods could enter the world again. As for being trapped there, I believe Ares and Aphrodite are lacking in their magic, and once they are strong enough, they won't be trapped in one world for long."

I shiver, thinking over that horrible thought. Hope still has more questions. "And were you originally from Earth? Born here?"

My grandmother picks up a teacup, her tea lukewarm now. She sips some before she talks. "No. We're from another world. A world where gods originated from. A few of us left and came to this world hundreds of years ago. We were searching for another, and many left. I decided to stay on Earth. So did many of the gods. But others, like Ares and Aphrodite, decided they needed a world they could conquer much more easily than Earth. People here don't believe so much in magic anymore, and our power is weak here. Ayiolyn is a world of magic, soaked rich in its land and people."

Hope continues, "Do you miss it? The world you're from?"

She smiles at her. I think she likes Hope, mostly because Hope is respectful to her, and it's the first time I've seen Hope be nice. "It's not much different to Ayiolyn. There are wolf shifters there, angels who feed off blood. There were a few gods there when we left, causing their own problems."

Livia smiles brightly. "Angels are real?"

"Yes. They have massive wings. The people of Lapetus believe in gods, the old ways and fated mates. Things that are not here on Earth any longer." My grandmother turns to me again. "Just come back, my granddaughter." She looks over her shoulder at Arty. "If the daughter of Aphrodite is lying about your mother, kill her. If she is not, tell your mother how much I love her and miss her."

Arty's eyes nervously flash but she stays silent with Kian at her side.

"I will."

She kisses my cheek once more, touching my

shoulder. I straighten my back and lift my head. It's time. "Are you coming, Arty?"

Arty whispers something to Kian, who holds her hand a little too long before letting her walk to the garden door.

"I'm not coming with you." We all turn to Livia, who shifts awkwardly, with Jinks by her feet, brushing his head against her leg, and I glare at him for a second. He looks right up at me, and I raise an eyebrow. He innocently meows. "I'm going to stay on Earth. I'm no use against the gods. I can't really fight, and I don't know the courts. There is nothing for me to do in that world to help you; I'd just be a liability. I wanted to get back to Earth, and now I'm back. I'm sorry, I just want to go back to my family."

I walk over and hug her tightly. "Thank you for being at my side for so long. It's not wrong for you to want to go home. Don't apologise to me. You're my friend."

"What about your dragon?" Hope snaps. "Do you think your dragon will be cool with you being a coward and running?"

Livia steps away from me. "I'm no coward, and my dragon would only be in danger trying to help me. This is how it's got to be," she says firmly. "I hope to see you again soon," she adds.

Hope huffs and turns away from her, her shoulders pulled tight.

"I'll help her find her family," my grandmother claims, placing her hand on Livia's arm.

"I should come with you," Kian states to Arty, a hint of possessiveness in his tone. He wants to keep her safe, even when he knows everything she has done. I don't know what to make of the strange thing going on between them.

"No," the queen all but shouts, stepping in front of her son. "Without Lysander, you are all that is left of the Water Court. They locked you up last time; they might use you against Lysander if they catch you again. Worse, they might kill you."

I meet his eyes, eyes so much like his brother's. Something cuts deep within my chest when I look at him. Something I'm not ready to admit. "She's right. I will find Lysander."

He looks at me suspiciously. "You hate him."

I wish it were that simple. "It's complicated, but no goddess gets to kill him."

It seems to quieten him, even as the queen steps closer to me. "What about the courts? The people? They are suffering."

Ayiolyn will always fight for you, but not yet. Live, and save our people one day. Remember, Ayiolyn is yours if you claim it. I blink, pushing back against my mother's words to me. "Those gods aren't meant to be in our world, and they've destroyed too much of it. My parents, my court, my people. I was a child the last time I was a Spirit Court princess, but I'm not anymore. I'm going to get it back, all of it, and make the gods regret coming into our world."

I walk past them into the garden, knowing I'm going to need a lot of space to pull in darkness to make a portal. I've never made one, but I understand the dynamics of it. I remember my father's lessons well. My father. I miss him so much. I hope, by using my Spirit Court power, I'm keeping a little of him alive. The proud, brilliant king I remember. All shadows can lead to all places, all worlds. I can connect through the darkness and shadows to worlds and places I know. I can weave them together and make a portal. I know I can. "I don't know how long I'll be able to open the portal for, so no messing about."

Hope and Arty stop at my side in the garden. "Are you going to think of your mother?" Arty suggests. "We need to go to the dungeons of the

Water Court castle and nowhere else, otherwise it's too much of a risk of someone seeing us."

I grit my teeth. "I've never been there, so it's going to be difficult to aim for the right place. My father always said, when you weave to places, you should only weave to the places you've been or you might end up in a wall or underwater. I was never taken to the Water Court as a child, let alone the dungeons."

Hope smirks. "I have. I've been there for years and know it very well. Can you see it in my mind? Hera obviously has power over minds, so you must have some of that power. You can look into my mind and see the Water Court. You can see the dungeons. You'll know exactly where to go that way."

Her plan would work, but... "I'm not very good at looking into minds. It'll hurt you. You will feel my powers invading your mind. My grandmother tried to teach me, but she said it takes hundreds of years to do it without causing a lot of pain."

Hope uncomfortably rubs her arm and blows out a breath. "Lysander, Arden, Grayson, and Emrys are the only family I have. I was brought up in the Water Court. There are people there who I care about. Just like in the other courts, too. A bit of pain for them, for the courts, I can do."

"It will be more than a bit." I frown.

She nervously laughs. "Let's admit it, you've always wanted to hurt me, you crazy bitch."

I almost laugh as I reach for her. "Still, I'm sorry." I touch the side of her face, and she screams. Images flash in my mind as the Water Court flashes through to me. I focus on the places, not her memories within them, and block her out. The throne room of the Water Court is clear first, a place of laughter and joy, and then she thinks of the entire castle. It's a massive greyish blue towering building above the sea. Sandy beaches are spread around one side, and the other is layered with stormy seas blowing harsh waves onto the cliffside. Two parts of the sea, vicious and calm, and it's all beautiful. All around the castle island are dozens, if not hundreds, of islands that probably make up the entire court. I watch in a haze as her memories slip through various rooms in the court in seconds until I see it, the dungeons, stretching out in front of me.

I lower my hand and she falls, collapsing to her knees with her long dark hair covering her face as I suck in a deep, shaky breath. I didn't just see her past, I felt some of her emotions, too. The lonesomeness, the desperation for family, the seeking of her past. It was intense, just like she is.

Arty catches her, but Hope pushes her away. "Don't touch me. I never want your help."

She throws her arms up. "I was just trying to help you up."

"I don't want help from someone like you," Hope snarls in return, and pain flashes across Arty's eyes. For a moment, I almost feel sorry for her, but then I remember the people she killed in the Dragon Crown Race. I remember her unlocking her father's cage and letting him free to murder hundreds of thousands. I remember her doing nothing as I was injured and thrown into a desert to die. I remember her betraying me at every chance she got. I offer Hope my hand, and she pulls herself up.

"Since when do you two get along?" Arty questions. "I thought Lysander—"

We both narrow our eyes on Arty, and she stops, and neither of us answers her. Hope looks at me, rubbing her forehead. "Did you see it? I have a headache now."

"Saw it. Everyone needs to be quiet and don't move." I close my eyes and reach for every bit of darkness, embracing it and sinking into the power like the feeling of coming home after a long day.

Darkness spreads across the ground, all the way up around us, like a curtain, taking out every light, every star. I pull the darkness from the shadows under the trees, the pitch-black pits in the soil of the earth and anything I can feel. I pull sharply, weaving it like it's a tapestry and pulling hundreds of the strands together with only one thought in my mind. One place. I weave them repeatedly, pushing and pulling, the pit of my power spreading. I focus on the Water Court, on the prisons, as I force my shadows to spread all the way there, through the worlds.

I open my eyes, praying this worked. A shimmering veil is in front of me, covered in water shadows. The water is pitch dark, different to portals I've seen before, but on the other side are the Water Court prisons. Relief floods me as I turn to Hope and nod once. Hope jumps through, with Arty following her, looking back at me once. I pray to every god out there, to the mighty dragon gods that I've never prayed to once before, that she's not going to betray me again.

I jump through the portal last, landing in soft water that climbs up to my knees. I leave the portal open for a while, just in case we need a fast escape, but it's quiet and empty. Deserted. The dungeons are dark and reek of damp, mould, and fish. There are a few glowing blue spheres lining the walls, and within them are glowing white fish, swimming round in circles.

Arty nods to her left, and I see a lump of someone lying on a watery bed, moss growing all around her long black hair. My heart is in my throat as I recognise my mother, and I stumble a step. I've not seen her in so long, and I thought she was dead. I never let myself hope, not even for a second, that I'd see her again. She's so pale, so thin and tiny. Her long hair spreads down her back, falling off the bed, and water drips off it into the puddles. She looks nothing like the healthy woman that the sorcerer made me see again and again, trying to get me to trust him all those months ago. It feels like a lifetime ago. No, this is my real mother, who's apparently been trapped down here.

I use my shadows to blast the prison door open as I run to her side. I push her onto her back, but her eyes stay closed, and she is floppy. "Mum!" I shake her shoulder, but she doesn't react. I turn to Arty. My eyes narrowed. "She's not waking up. What's wrong with her?!"

Arty holds her hands up, nervously looking at the snakes of shadows lacing around the corners of the room. "I d-don't know. She never wakes anymore. I think it must be a spell of some kind. My nanny, Tara, a spelled human, comes down to care for her and makes sure she is having some food and water. But she told me she doesn't eat or drink anymore, the last few weeks."

I look at the portal, making a new plan. "We send her back to Earth, to my grandmother."

Hope nods at me before turning to Arty. "Watch the door and make sure no one comes in."

"No one will come down here. There are no other prisoners," she whispers. "Father kills or spells anybody who fights him. He doesn't keep them prisoners anymore. Prince Kian was kept down here, but Father's not even noticed he's missing yet. Or he definitely would have been searching for him."

"Still, watch the door," Hope snaps.

I touch my mother's hand, running my fingers over the silver dragon bracelet on her wrist. The memories of when I played with it all the time rush back to me, and I remember hoping one day she would let me wear it. I gulp down the emotions running to the surface, knowing I can't lose it here. I have to be strong. "Thank you for coming to me, for telling me about my mother. Artemis, I might never trust you again as my friend, but I am thankful for this."

"I will keep earning your trust. I'm done being a slave to my parents when I know they don't love me." She lifts her head with every word. Arty walks to the door, her back to us.

Hope comes over, kneeling and looking at me. "She's still breathing, and that's all that matters. Your mum's alive." I don't know how she knew I needed to hear that, but I did.

"Alive," I breathe the word out as I rise to my feet. With Hope's help, we carry my mum through the portal and lay her down on the grass in the garden, sending my shadows to lead grandmother outside to her in a second. I lean down to my mum. "I'm going to save our court and free our people. I'm going to save Ayiolyn, just like you taught me to." I shakily kiss her cheek before going back into the portal with Hope and letting it close behind me, leaving my family in another world. They are safe, I remind myself.

Terrin's relief floods my mind as he senses me back in this world. "You're alive," he whispers to me, his voice broken. "You should not be in this world. It is falling, my rider."

"And you should not make a choice for me to

leave without asking me if I wanted to or not. I'm furious at you and them, but right now, I need you to fly to me."

"On my way," he simply replies, sounding like he wants to say more. I cut him off, knowing I can't argue with him about it all right now.

I look at Hope and Arty, the only ones I have to trust in this castle for everything to work out. "Now, we get our courts back and save the kings."

CHAPTER 2

ARTEMIS

No one watches me in the corridors, and it's a blessing. I'm a shadow to them, which in all honesty, is perfect for me right at this moment. I've always been a shadow to my parents, and I understand it. I might be the daughter of two powerful Greek gods, but I don't have any magic, not even a drop, and they make sure everyone knows I'm not a threat. Still, the people of the Water Court keep a good distance from me, from everyone, as they make their way down the pathways of the castle.

This castle is alive, the very walls seem to be listening, and I swear they guide me to the room quicker than I ever have been before. I make my way into the side room of the chambers of the throne, a public room that is now completely empty except for the book that my mother has left out for anyone who dares to sign. The door opens for me, and I slip inside, my breaths coming out in clouds. I don't know if the castle can hear me, what magic it really holds, but I whisper, "Please let me know if anyone is coming."

In response, the door lock clicks shut behind me. I grin. It feels too easy as I push my back against the cold door, listening to the sounds of the guards walking the corridor outside and the echo of the sea outside the castle. It's cold, empty, and silent in this place. I remember the stories my nanny Tara, a spelled mortal tasked with bringing me up in mortal ways, told me of the joyful Water Court. She lived here for a time with one of the water queens, but she was from Earth. The court used to be full of water creatures, splendid feasts, and art displays. Now…anything good like that has been drained away.

I nervously glance around the room for a minute, making sure I'm alone before walking to the book. The book is simple, with a feather pen resting on the tip of it, and I feel nothing strange from it like magic. I quickly write her name on the paper, just like she asked me to: Princess Ellelin

Spirit Ilroth of the Fifth Court. My heart is racing as I put the pen down, noticing there's not a single other name signed in the book. I don't blame them. Even being queen of the Water Court is not worth being under the gods' control like slaves. Anyone who signs this, they know they're signing up to be a prisoner, unless they're extremely powerful or stupid, which few are.

It surprises me how many are loyal to the kings, no matter what my father or mother does to them. They remain loyal. Many screamed that it's the Dragon Crown Race that chooses the queen, even right before my father killed them.

They will kill me when they know what I've done. I rush out of the room with that thought, slipping back into the corridor. I've made so many mistakes, listened to my parents' every word, and never once thought for myself until Kian showed me to be better. I can die my own person, which makes me richer than I ever have been before. I hope this is a step towards redeeming some of the horrors of my past.

I rub my cheek as I stroll to my room, finding Tara sitting on a chair in the corner, stitching a dress. Tara has rich wrinked skin, light brown hair that she keeps in a bob under her ears, and she always wears colourful patterned dresses that make her eyes sparkle. Her dark brown eyes brighten when she sees me, and she opens her arms. I don't hesitate before running into her arms, one of the few bits of comfort I ever get. "My darling Artemis, you look pale. Are you well?"

"I'm fine, it's just been a strange few weeks with them both here and free." I pause. Tara knows how I really feel about my parents, and she has always supported me and protected me however she can. I've asked more than once about her life before my parents took her and forced her to work for them, but she only ever said everyone who meant something is long gone for her. Only I remained now. Tara brought me up to be good, and I didn't become what she wanted in the end. I can see it now, the slight disappointment in her eyes. "I preferred it when they pretended that I didn't exist and left us alone."

Her brow creases. "Arty," she whispers, the nickname she gave me in secret. My parents hated the nickname whenever I asked them to call me by it. She looks like she is about to say something, something important, but my door is yanked open.

I turn to see a guard, the dark blue armour shining. "Artemis, you've been called to the court by your parents. Come." The guard has icy blue eyes, white hair, and a red haze to his eyes that suggests he's completely and utterly under my mother's spell. She spelled the ones that would not help and killed the ones that were too strong for the spells. Some of the court is not spelled, and they choose to stay. This guard, something about his face shape reminds me of Lysander, and I wonder if he is some kind of relative. I nod before standing. I look down at Tara. "I love you. I'll come and see you when I can."

"I love you too, darling," she gently replies, and I grin at her. I feel her eyes on me all the way out of the room, and I struggle to keep up with the guard and his giant footsteps. My ribs are still broken, and I'm bruised far too much to be running with him. My father was especially brutal the last time I saw him, and every inch of me wants to run in the other direction rather than come to their call. I'm trapped, but not for long. Ellelin is here, and things are going to change.

I felt something different the moment I met Ellelin, and not because I knew who she was and what I needed to do but because she is so determined. My father gave me simple instructions: take Ellelin's blood after she was my friend, so the blood was willingly given as per the curse's instructions, and kill all of the other competitors. I could have poisoned them all, killed them in their sleep, done a number of things on the first night, but I didn't. My father was furious at me for changing my mind and claiming that it wasn't easy to get Ellelin to be my friend, when in truth, she was my friend from the beginning. I was myself with her, the girl Tara brought me up to be, with all the human parts of Tara that she taught me. Not the monster my father commanded me to be.

I wish I could change things and not let fear control my decisions like I did.

As we weave through the castle, it's silent. Far too silent. As I turn into the throne room, the guard remains at the door, and I know why the castle is pretty empty. The throne room is flooded with people from the court, a wave of blue dresses and suits on either side of the pathway to the thrones. Their heads are bowed and not one of them dares look up or make a sound, not even the children or babies I spot mothers holding.

My mother and father are sitting on the thrones, lounging on them, like they are meant to be there, when everyone else in this room knows they are not. Imposters. My father's staff is spread across his lap, and he taps his fingers on it as I approach. On either side of my parents are the dragon kings on their knees, and they are broken. A red glaze covers their eyes, and thick chains are wrapped around their wrists. They're under my mother's spell and they don't move. There's a feeling of hopelessness echoing around the room, and it threatens to suck me into it. Ellelin. Ellelin is coming. The princess of the only court my father fears is here.

My mother waves me over. She is wearing a thin red gown, her legs crossed, revealing a deep slit up her leg, showing all of her golden skin. Her long blonde hair falls down to her waist, and every bit of her sparkles like she is the sun. Beautiful, but unlike the sun, she is empty and cold inside. "Where have you been?"

"Just around," I lie. I lie well. She taught me that.

My mother rolls her eyes. "It's an important day, and yet no one has signed up for the tests." She looks at me. "I was thinking, and perhaps you could sign up."

My heart races. "Why would I do that?"

She leans forward, a look nothing short of malice in her eyes because I've dared to challenge her. "We need people to be enticed to sign up. It seems that my test wasn't that popular, and I want to play a game. I'm bored. Do I need to convince you to do as I ask?"

"Love of mine," my father interrupts, touching her bare leg. She faces him. "Why would you be bored? Everything is in our palms in this world, and there's no one to oppose us. The dragons of the West have gone completely silent, hidden with their dragons' tails between their legs. The idea of beating us is gone, and we will destroy them soon enough. Our magic is growing and soon we will be able to open a portal to another world, for more wa—"

She places her finger on his lips. "You are the god of war. I am the goddess of love. War does not interest me, it bores me. All that death and for no good reason." She flicks her thick locks of hair over her shoulder and looks at me again. "So, do you need convincing?"

A cry reaches me, and I turn, my eyes widening as Tara is dragged into the room by two guards. They dump her in front of my mother. "WAIT! NO!" I can't do anything, I'm not fast enough, and I have no power to stop my mother from wrapping red magic like a cloud around Tara and draining the life from her as I run to stop it. She knows I love

Tara, she can sense it, and love is a weapon she uses against everyone. Even her own daughter. When I get close, she drops Tara on the stone like she is nothing and sighs as I grab her shoulders, pulling her onto my lap, knowing she is going to die. "No, no, no, no." I cry, hot tears falling down my cheeks and a sob echoing in my throat. I can barely see through the tears, my heart breaking.

My mother sighs. "Honestly, she was just staff and a pointless mortal. Why are you crying over her? I named you after my friend, a powerful goddess, and here you are, powerless and pointlessly crying over a mortal's death."

I weep as I hold Tara to me, hearing her crackled whisper in my ear. "You are not powerless, my darling Arty. Prove to them how good you are, and I will see you in the skies with the mighty dragon gods of this world."

A scream escapes my throat as she goes still in my arms, her chest freezing along with what feels like time as the room goes still. I'm done with my parents; I'm never, ever helping them. I'm going to make sure Ellelin wins and my parents die. I barely notice the shadows spread across the room, washing around my legs and Tara's body at first. My father shouts, "What is happening? Who is doing that?"

Shadows spread everywhere until massive dark wings made of shadows shift into the shape of a dragon appearing over the throne room. It crashes down, ripping off the roof of the throne room, sending stone everywhere as people run out of the room screaming. Ellelin, riding a massive shadow dragon with wings bigger than any dragon I've ever seen, lands in the middle of the throne room. The dragon disappears around her, letting her gently fall down to her feet in a cloud of darkness. It disappears in the air, and for a moment, she looks like she has shadow wings spreading out of her back. Ellelin is in black armour and tight-fitting black clothes with the Spirit Court dragon symbol on her chest plate. She just needs her crown now.

My father stands, lifting up his staff, instantly throwing magic straight at her. Only for it to simply bounce away, unable to touch her at all. He looks at her in pure confusion and complete fear. Something about the fifth court scares him, and I'm going to find out what that is. "That's impossible!" he roars.

My mother laughs and laughs. "Stupid spirit girl, you signed up for my test! The one that offered pure protection from both of us?" She claps. "Very smart or idiotic. You did it in the name of love, and I admire that."

"What have you done?" my father all but growls at Aphrodite, grabbing her wrist.

She roughly tugs her wrist out of his grip. "How was I to know she'd do this?"

The princess of the Spirit Court stands in front of the gods and makes one single claim that shakes this realm. "They belong to me, not you. You will give them back, or your world is going to drown in my darkness."

CHAPTER 3

Shadows spread around me like small rivers, mixing and spreading into every inch of the Water Court throne room. They continue spinning around the cold, damp air that tastes and smells like sea water. None of the people of the Water Court are hurt as my dragon disappears into the void of darkness and shadow, waiting once more for me to call. The throne room is more than I expected it to be, with huge waterfalls down each wall, creating steady streams of blue water within the stone pathways. Some guards barely get two steps closer before I throw them into the walls with my shadows and hold them there. The rest of them step back, their weapons dropping to the ground. Dragon roars echo outside the castle, but they reach us all, and I wonder if they are roaring for me or for the gods sitting on their king's throne.

I barely noticed Ares and Aphrodite on the throne, which is buried in an archway at the back of the room, with four short blue stone steps leading up to it. Her laughter echoes around the room as my entire focus shifts onto the only men I have ever loved. My dragon kings. My chest hurts, my heart slamming so hard that it feels like it will beat itself out of rhythm. They're kneeling in puddles of water. Each one of them has a completely blank expression, their eyes covered in a red haze. They look black and blue with bruises, but they are alive. Relief threatens to pull me to my knees. The gods haven't killed them. Even when every inch of me is desperate to run to them, to open a portal and bring us all to Earth to escape, I hold still. That plan would not work and it's too risky.

I'm signed up for a magical test, once again, but this time I've joined willingly. I watch them with every bit of hope, longing, anger, and pain that I could feel. I hope they are aware of what is happening, that they know I'm here to help them and get them out of whatever curse they're under. I straighten my shoulders, pulling my eyes from my dragon kings with all the strength I've got left.

Facing Aphrodite and Ares is easier than the men I'm in love with, who dragged us all into this mess. They are waiting for me to acknowledge them. "How did you survive?" he asks.

I turn my gaze to him. Ares's long green cloak covers the throne room seat, his staff resting in hand, ready to be used. He murdered my father, killed hundreds of people in my court, and tried to conquer this world. I lost everything because of him. I don't care if he is a god; he is fucking dead. "Ares." He frowns. "My grandmother, Hera, explained to me who you really are. She sends her wishes for your long, painful death at my hand."

His eyes narrow. "I prefer the title sorcerer, and your grandmother is a fool, trapped in a magicless world." He is practically shaking with anger. "You made a grave mistake turning up here and signing up for that test. I'm guessing my worthless daughter had something to do with it."

I follow his gaze to Arty, who's on her knees, holding a dead woman to her chest, crying her eyes out. I didn't kill the woman, and I don't know who that is, but her cries are nothing short of losing someone she loves. She barely even lifts her head at her father's mention of her name, but her voice echoes as she proclaims, "I stand with the fifth court, and the true princess."

Ares throws shadows her way, but I block them before he can hit her, a clash of light and shadow exploding between us all. Arty doesn't move, and she continues to cling to the dead woman. Aphrodite stands, her long red gown pooling onto the steps as she walks down to me. She looks over her shoulder.

"That's enough, husband. It seems our daughter is under the princess of the Spirit Court's spell," she says before turning to me. "Such strange, curious, and powerful magic. I can see it all around you." She pauses on the last step so she is standing over me. We both know she purposely stopped there. I try not to look at my dragon kings while she is watching me so closely. "No wonder you found four kings to love you. They are devoted. It is impressive."

There is silence when no one replies to her, and I won't give her the satisfaction of an answer. She twirls a lock of her glistening blonde hair. "No one signed up for my test other than you, and I'm guessing no one will now. Who would want to compete with the princess of the strongest court? So, let's make a deal?"

I look into her eyes, making sure she sees me. Making sure she understands the lengths I am willing to go to save them. My life...I don't want it if they don't survive. "I want my dragon kings and the courts back."

She finally gives up the step to walk around me, but she doesn't touch me, although I keep my shadows at bay just in case. I don't trust her word, her spells, or tests. "Did you learn the conditions of my deal with the fire king?" She raises an eyebrow when I silently nod. "If any decided to take you as their mates, this would never have happened. Aren't you upset with them?"

I curl my hands into fists. "They're mine, and I didn't come here to discuss my feelings with you."

Her laugh is enchanting as it echoes. "All of this is about your feelings. Love is endless and stupid, or you would not be here." She grins widely. "I'm the goddess of love. I can see the bonds of love. The echoes of love that have only just begun are like strings, and I have the power to tug on them as I see fit. I can see traces in the air that bind strangers who haven't even met yet, and if I wish, I can pull two strangers onto one path." She leans in, her voice a whisper. "I see your feelings, princess. They're your mates, aren't they? Fate has bound you to four powerful kings. Your bond is strong and clear with one, but the others you have not bonded with yet. It's all so interesting."

"What is the point of all this?" Ares snaps, slamming his staff on the ground, cracking the stone. "Just end her! You made this foolish—"

"I am getting to my point," Aphrodite interrupts with a smile of pure seduction flashed at her husband, which drops when she looks my way. "You love them, and love is a weapon I wield the best. It has always been interesting to me what people wouldn't do for love. The poets have always claimed that it's one of the greatest weapons known to humans. It's also one of the greatest weapons known to us. To gods. To demigods like yourself. To possessive dragons."

"Stop playing games, my wife," Ares warns, "and just kill her."

Aphrodite rolls her eyes. "The game has begun, my husband, and nothing will stop it. She has my full protection from everybody, including myself. I cannot kill her."

"Then I'll order a guard too!" he shouts, full of frustration.

I hold my hand up, shadows wrapping around my fingers. "Do you really think a guard would be able to stop me? Don't bother." I pull shadows around me. "You killed my entire court, and you should be more concerned about what is stopping me from attacking you."

"If you touch my husband or me, I will kill your dragon kings with the click of my fingers," Aphrodite interrupts. I drop my powers, my shadows leaving. I see a bit of Arty in her face, in her expressions, as she faces me. They have the same classic beauty in some lights, but her beauty is rotten. Aphrodite is alluring, seductive, but dead inside. She isn't going to make any of this easy for me. "As you can see, they're under my spell. My curse, so to speak. It can't be broken unless I wish it. I will give you them back for each test, and if you win, you keep what is left. If any of them die, I win."

"That easily?" I question. I notice Arty pulling the body of the woman away and out the side door. Her parents don't notice her leave. Aphrodite grins before she leaves me to sit back on the throne. "This throne should be yours, destined mate of the Water Court king. There's some irony in the fact you are down there, begging for help."

I lift my head. "What do you want in return for the spell being broken and the safety of the courts?"

Aphrodite runs her hand down the arm of the throne. "We continue on with my game and the plan that I set up. One test, in each of the courts, and we will travel between them. You can finally see the courts you haven't seen since you were a child as we conquer them. This will be entertainment for us while we wait."

"What kind of tests?" I demand.

"In the court of Water, a monster lurks.

In the court of Fire, flames burn away any lies.

In the court of Earth, touch is key.

In the court of Air, try to breathe.

These are your hints, but I will not tell you more." She watches me as I take in her cryptic poem and try to work out what any of the tests could be. I don't like the sound of the first one. A monster? Fucking brilliant. "Our deal will go like this. If you win, then you get them back, court by court. Dragon by dragon. With each win, the court will be yours to rule. We will leave the court alone."

"Are you out of your fucking mind?" Ares roars, grabbing her arm. "I am not giving up—"

She puts her hand over his, and he stops mid-sentence. I'm somewhat impressed that she managed to stop the god of war with just a hand. Is she more powerful than him? "And if you lose, all of the magic of the spirit is ours. This would mean the instant death of your cursed dragons. Yes, we know about that. Whispers fly around here."

My heart near enough stops as she continues. "You will essentially kill anybody that's in your court if you lose."

Terrin. All of the dragons that are cursed, that I promised to free at some point. My people, who my father sacrificed so much to keep safe. If I lose, they die. If I refuse her, my dragon kings and their courts die. There'd be no going home for any of us. Both choices are curses. I glance at them, and I know my answer because it's selfish. It's not the answer of a ruler. It's the answer of someone that's completely in love. There is nothing I wouldn't try for them, nothing that I wouldn't do. I hate that they put me in this position. If only my dragon kings had spoken to me, done anything other than this. We could have avoided every horror I'm about to sign up for. I'm so tired, so tired of fighting and surviving and nothing more.

"I want you to promise that my dragon kings will not be hurt while the tests continue. Arty is also to be left alone," I add in. She is the reason I even knew about this and had a chance.

Aphrodite nods. "You have a deal." She claps,

and power echoes in the room as red fog rolls in through the ceiling. Ares is quiet, far too quiet, as he sits beside her. When he sees me looking, he meets my eyes and smirks.

That alone makes my stomach sink. I'm playing a game of the gods, and I know they are going to try to screw me over. Aphrodite's magic spreads around me, and it lifts my arm into the air. "I will mention, for words have certain power when it comes to this kind of magic, that during the test, you are forbidden to use your powers."

"NO!" I shout, but it's too late. I scream as her magic rips into my skin, leaving markings in the shape of chains wrapped around my hand. Each one has a symbol of an element shining within the lock of the chain on my palm. Water is at the top. She looks at Lysander. As he rises to his feet, his eyes still hazy, he looks right through me with every step. My water king, my enemy, and I'm happy to see him coming to me despite everything. I couldn't be more furious at him, at them all, but us staying alive is more important right now. He stops right in front of me, towering so tall I arch my neck to look up at him, wishing I could see his green eyes. His red hair is wavy around his stupidly handsome face.

"You will go together, and we will watch. What do the humans say? Good luck."

A portal opens right beneath us, and I immediately plummet through the air, screaming into nothing. I desperately reach out for Lysander, but he's ripped away from me within moments. All I see is the cold wash of a giant wave as it slams right into me, and then—bang! My head hits a rock.

CHAPTER 4

My body awakens to the taste of salt water and the thunderous sound of waves. My eyes widen in shock as a wave crashes into me with overwhelming strength, plunging me under the bitter cold salt water that burns my eyes when I force them open. I swim back up to the surface, my muscles aching as I spin around, looking for something. There is a huge, jagged rock sticking out of the sea next to me, and I must have hit my head on it and somehow stayed alive. My purple-dipped, wet locks of hair are wrapped around my neck and face, and I push them away to see better.

Everything is fuzzy as I see a floating tree trunk, and I dive for it. Several waves, not as big as the first one, push into me and make the trunk float further away each time I'm close. I'm exhausted, cold, and angry by the time I can grab the floating piece of trunk. I pull myself onto it, lying down as it floats through the sea, somehow skirting over the waves. I can't stop shaking as I touch my head, pulling my hand away and seeing red blood coating my fingers. I barely get a chance to look up before another giant wave slams into me and snaps the trunk in half, throwing me back into the water.

Lightning flashes across the sky, and I gasp, taking in water, coughing on it as I break the surface. I reach for my powers on instinct, wanting to help myself, but Aphrodite was right. She took them. The storms, the waves, all of it becomes a mild threat when I feel something brush against my legs. Looking down, I see something bright gold as it flashes past me. My blood runs cold as I try to stay still and silent as the massive creature swims away. At least I'm not alone. "Massive sea creature" wasn't exactly on my list of helpful friends here though. But it hasn't tried to eat me, so I'm hoping it's not on the people-eating monster list.

Lysander would know. Lysander. He is here somewhere, and he can't be dead…I'd know it. I'd feel it. He is my destined mate after all, and despite how much I hate him, I need him right now.

"LYSANDER!" I scream his name, searching in the dark seas for him, a new desperation to find him washing away all my fears. He doesn't shout back, no one answers me. Calm. I have to calm down, even if it feels like my soul might leave my body in pure fear. I spin in the sea, letting the waves move me along in the water, but there's nothing but water in every direction. I'm floating, lost, and failing this test. I'm failing my people. "LYSANDER!" I scream his name over and over, hoping that he'll hear me, hoping he'll call back. But between the blistering icy rain, the sea waves, and the storm, I'm not sure I'd even hear him. I shout through our bond, but he is silent. Too silent for Lysander. Even he wouldn't let me die here and ignore me. I hope.

Essentially, I should be able to find him anywhere with this bond. With every bit of strength I have, I close my eyes and let everything leave my mind except for him. I picture him in front of me, his dark red hair, devastatingly beautiful features, muscular body, his evil smile. I can feel him, like a string vibrating alongside my own soul. In all this madness, knowing that a creature of the sea could eat me at any second, that I'd be screwing over my entire court if I lose, I feel him. He's near me.

Determination burns in my mind as I open my eyes, suck in a deep breath, and begin to swim. The waves are against me, the very sea parting us, but I don't give up. The tugging sensation is like a flutter in my chest, pulling me to follow it, promising me he will be on the other end. With everything I have, I keep swimming in that direction even as wave after wave hits me. My heart leaps when I spot something in the distance, floating face down in the water. Lysander. As I near him, I see that he is actually flung over the side of what looks like a mini-island of moss, only big enough to hold him on it. His red hair is like a beacon to me, and my shoulders drop. I found him.

I dive to him, pushing against the sea to let me get to my Lysander. My arms ache when I finally get close enough to grab the rocky island he is on and pull myself up next to him. I shake his shoulder, pulling him onto his back. I can't name the relief I feel when I see his chest moving up and down. He's alive. He's actually alive. There is blood on the rocks, and he must have landed here. My relief is soon tempered by anger. "Lysander, wake the fuck up!"

He wakes up, opening his eyes, and for a moment I almost forgot the spell he was under. But there is no redness in his eyes. It's gone, and when he sees me, he smiles for just a second. Just as a wave is going to hit us, Lysander grabs me tightly around my waist and makes walls of water spiral around us, protecting us in a spinning cyclone. The wave just crashes against it, spraying us with droplets. Lysander touches my forehead, frowning. His magic washes over the cut, soothing me. "You need to stop injuring yourself, witch." I huff out a laugh, pulling back from him. His eyes are like glowing green crystals, and they are full of disappointment. "What the fuck are you doing here, Ellelin?"

He rarely uses my full name, and red clouds my vision as I glare at him. Even when I'm stuck in the middle of the sea, no thanks to him, he is telling me off. I scream in frustration and slam my hand into his shoulder. "What am I doing here? I am fixing your fucked-up mistakes! This"—I wave around me—"is all your fault. And theirs. How dare you make up a crazy ass plan to just leave me on Earth? What did you think would happen? Do you think I'd be able to live knowing you were on Ayiolyn, suffering or dead? Do you think I'd be okay with that? What life did you think I'd ever be able to have?"

"We—"

I slam my hand into his chest this time, stopping him, my hot tears falling down my cheeks. "I made my choice, back in the desert, back in the courts, that I am from this world, and I am not choosing a normal human life. I couldn't just go and live on Earth, pretending I am not in love with the kings of another world." I slam my other hand into his chest. "Do you know how worried I was when I woke up without you four? How fucking scared I was for you? I've had to process everything that happened to me while coming back here, fighting for you, and fixing your mistakes. I've had to make a deal with Aphrodite for the lives of my entire court and all my magic. Just because you guys wouldn't speak to me, wouldn't include me, and chose to be the heroes that no one asked for!"

I smack my hands over and over on his chest, unable to see through my tears.

"Ellelin—"

"NO!" I shout. "How dare you do that to me? I needed you after... I needed you." I pause, actually looking at him. Lysander looks devastated. "I needed you. Even when I hate you sometimes, I needed you." He pulls me to his chest even as I fight him, until I'm a shaking mess in his arms, clinging to his shirt as he holds me tightly against the storms as we rock in the sea.

When there is nothing but the sound of a storm, he kisses me softly on top of my head. "I'm sorry." I don't think I've ever heard him say those words before. I didn't know he was capable of them. "You don't hate me anymore, and I never hated you. But I fucked up everything, over and over, and saying sorry is the only way I know how to begin to fix it all. I wanted to do that since the night I found you injured. Something broke in me that night, and I wish I could go back and tell myself to admit it. In my soul, I suspected that you're my mate, but I had no proof. I didn't know we were mind speaking like destined mates, but I was curious how it was possible. I felt your fear when you were drowning, and for a moment, I thought of how water could take you from me, and I hated it. I hated water, my power, my court, for daring to take air from your lungs. Even before that, even when I convinced myself that I felt nothing for you, I was obsessed with keeping you safe. I wouldn't have touched your grandmother, and revenge went on the back burner in my mind."

I lift my head up. "When Arden told me of the deal he made to get us out, the deal with Aphrodite, I agreed with it before even thinking. Emrys came up with the plan to get you back to Earth, like you asked for from the moment we kidnapped you."

"Things changed."

He looks up, rain dripping down his face. When he looks down at me, I feel like the world stops. "I wanted you to have a normal life, away from us all, if it was on Earth or not. But fuck, did I want a life with you more. I would fight for a life with you, for a moment with you, just anything you are willing to give me. You're my enemy, my spirit witch, and I'm in fucking love with you."

"Lysander—"

"I don't expect you to say it back, not even for a second, because I fucked up in every inch of our relationship. I can't speak for the others, but I shouldn't have lied to you about all of this. We should be in there together, and if you would give me a chance, I will drown this world to fix it for you."

"Drowning seems pretty easy at the moment," I manage to say. I can't say what he wants me to, not right now, not with how angry I still am at him. We have too much to discuss, Arden for starters, and how he thinks my father killed his.

"You're safe with me, even if we are in a storm in the middle of one of the most fucking dangerous seas in Ayiolyn. I would use my power toward just a few seconds of peace with you any moment, any time, in any world." My heart races. Lysander never speaks to me like this, and I'm starting to think he is more dangerous when he is being seductive than he is when he is being cruel.

"You've changed, my enemy."

He grins at me, holding me closer. His hand sinks into my hair, pulling us closer. "I'm done pushing you away. I am done pretending like you aren't everything to me. We're gonna fight our way out of this. We'll win this test and show the gods they have nothing on dragons. Dragons rule."

He moves us so close I can taste him on my every breath. "I'm no dragon."

Lysander's lips tilt but his eyes are filled with determination. "I saw you on the shadow dragon. Every bit of a spirit princess of the fifth court dragons. You are a dragon, my spirit witch." He leans into me, and my breath halts. "I'm going to kiss you and never let you go. You need to push me away if you're not ready—"

I kiss him. I kiss my enemy like he isn't my enemy at all and, instead, he is my entire world. His lips press harshly against mine in return, an echo of a groan vibrating up his throat that I feel in my blood. Lysander brutally kisses me, a desperate rush to take as much of me as he can with just his mouth. Just for a moment, the world blurs, and he makes me feel like I'm alive. I wasn't sure I'd be able to kiss him after everything, but it feels easy. Natural to kiss my destined mate, someone born for me as much as I was born for him. Our past, our arguments and fights, are a memory for a few seconds as I sink into his hard body, rain still pouring on us, reminding me that we're still in danger. I can taste him on my lips as I break away from him. He reaches for me again, but I place my hand on his chest. "What did you mean when you talked about the most dangerous sea in Ayiolyn?"

"I haven't been back here in years. My father used to bring us here as a test for royals when I was a kid," he answers, so casually that he barely registers the look of horror on my face.

A tic in his jaw twitches as my words wash over him like smoke. "How old were you?" How could his father bring him here, to this horrid place?

"Young," he sharply answers, and he looks

away, letting me go. He isn't going to talk to me about it, not right now at least. I push the knowledge to the back of my mind.

"What's wrong with these seas?" I ask.

"It's full of monsters that are kept away from the islands, and the sea is known to destroy ships and life. Giant sea creatures dwell in the depths that make dragons look like toys for a child. This is the only part of the sea that doesn't abide by my rule. It's too wild, too unkept, and no king has ever been able to claim these seas or the monsters within. I believe my great-grandfather tried once, but he was eaten." My eyes widen. That must have been one crazy bastard. "But to survive the seas means you are a true king. I used to be left out here for weeks, and I know there are little islands around. They appear and disappear on the tides. We need to make our way to one of them…" He keeps talking, making his plan, but I'm stuck on the fact his father left him out here for weeks as a young child. Lysander finally looks at me, and his eyes narrow. "I don't want your pity."

I try to hide my emotions, knowing we need to work together. "Right. How are we going to get to an island? Can you shift? I haven't got my powers, or I would call my shadows."

He smirks at me. "My dragon is blocked by that bitch goddess, but I'm the fucking king of the Water Court. Ruler of the seas, the oceans, the rivers, and you are mine. I will get us out of here."

Pure possessiveness flashes in the depths of his eyes. I'm still angry at him. I think I'll be angry for years to come for what they have done, but I don't correct his claim. I'm his, we both know it. He is mine too. We might die together at any moment, and I'd rather not die completely hating him. Plus, it wasn't just him that made that choice. I'm furious at all of them. "Stay on the turtle." Lysander touches the island. "Thank you for saving me, friend."

"It's a turtle?!" I shout as he makes a gap in the water shield around us. Lysander doesn't answer me as he suddenly jumps off the turtle, diving into the sea, leaving me behind. The turtle moves up, revealing more of the shell, and its purple head pops above the water. It looks right at me, and a sound like a whale cry sings from its throat. It's a beautiful noise. I touch its back. "Thank you for helping us."

The song continues, even as the turtle looks away from me. Waiting and waiting, I watch the sea through the gap, the violent waves and flashes of pure lightning that highlight nothing but the dark rain clouds. It's been too long. I stand up, ready to dive into the sea for him if he doesn't appear soon. I step back as something crashes out of the ocean, flashes of gold flooding my vision. A giant creature lands on the water outside the gap, and it looks like a water snake had a baby with an eel made of gold. Small whiskers that buzz with electricity fill the water at its sides, and sitting on its back between its humps is Lysander. He wipes his hair from his face, his other hand holding into a leash made of seaweed. He offers me his hand. "Come on, witch."

I raise an eyebrow and he laughs as a wave of water swiftly lifts me up in the air and throws me at him. Lysander catches me too easily and slides me in front of him. "You're insane!"

"And you are beautiful."

I'm stunned for a second at his compliment, but my eyes widen as the whiskers of the creature lift, spreading out and revealing webbing between them. All of that looks like wings. Lysander wraps his arm tight around my body as the golden creature dives in the water, pulling us both down with it, and I clutch Lysander's arm tightly. It crashes out of the sea again, right up into the air, and starts flying straight up into the sky. It dives through the storm cloud, right into pure, warm sunlight. I look back at Lysander, the burnt orange and sunflower yellow rays of the sun making his hair look like the beginning of a fire. "The sea is not your enemy, Elle. You were born to be the queen of it."

"I would disagree about it being my enemy," I grumble, making him laugh. I grin as the creature shoots through the sky, any warmth from the sun departing in the icy wind. A piercing noise, like a musical trill echoes out of its throat as it flies high. I miss the sweet turtle singing. We fly around for a bit, and I shiver, leaning back into the warmth of Lysander. I'm not sure we have a destination in mind, but suddenly the creature dives through the clouds, my stomach swirling from the drop. Lightning flashes near us, and I can barely hold on as the creature moves faster. As we break out of the storm clouds, I see a small island with nothing but sand and two windswept trees. Lysander lands the creature on the beach, and it waits for him in the water after we have climbed off.

I sit on the sand, pulling my knees up, my wet clothes sticking to me. Lysander chooses to stand, watching the seas. "There's got to be a test here. Can't just be survival."

"Agreed," I answer, but I'm clueless what to suggest the answer is. Eventually Lysander sits with me, and I build a sand castle. He kicks it with his foot. "You're mean."

"Never claimed not to be," he answers, but he is smiling. It's weird to see him smile so much. For a while, we sit on the beach together and just watch the giant ocean storms, the waves bigger than houses, swallowing up everything in their way. I want to ask about his father, but I know now's not the time. I feel like him admitting any of that to me is enough. It's a step in the right direction.

When dawn starts to break around the horizon, light crashes through the storms of clouds like beacons. But it's not the light that makes my blood run cold. An overly sweet female voice fills my mind. "Save the seven betrayers. If any are lost, so will you be."

I rush to my feet, right before I see a whirlpool in the sea and hear a monster roar that makes me clamp my hands over my ears. I spot flashing red lights in several places around the seas. Lysander isn't looking at me, but he is pale. Where the red flashes were, small boats are floating, being sucked into the pull of a whirlpool. "It isn't a whirlpool, but it's the Charybdis."

"What is a Charybdis?" I quietly ask.

Lysander finally looks at me, and I don't like the

fear in his eyes. "It's like a worm with a lot of teeth that lives in water, and it eats everything. It can't be reasoned with, and it's told as horror stories in my court. I wasn't aware it was even real. I won't take you out there."

"No." I touch his arm. "We go together. I know it's risky, but what she said? Seven betrayers? That's people out there on those boats, and we need to get to them. Don't leave me behind again."

He tenses, but his shoulders drop. "Fine, but will you do everything I tell you?"

I smile. "Just this once."

Lysander kisses me quickly. "I wouldn't expect anything less."

I climb up onto the golden creature after Lysander, and he takes off straight into the skies. The first boat is nearest, with a dark-haired woman trying to wiggle out of rope tied around her arms. Lysander growls. "She's from my court, a good friend of my mother's. These are all high nobles of my court. What's left of them."

Aphrodite called them betrayers. They betrayed her and Ares's rule, not Lysander. This is what is left of the high nobles of the Water Court. Lysander swoops the creature low enough before I jump off. I pull at the rope binding her until it's off her, and she meets my eyes. "Thank you to you both, the true rulers of water."

"Climb on," I gently instruct her, noticing how she looks weak, too weak to even stand. Lysander pulls her behind him before helping me back on. One down, six to go. Thankfully, the boats are spread out and pretty far from the Charybdis. The whirlpool it is creating is pulling them in, bit by bit, and we don't have long.

The woman is silent as we go from boat to boat, untying and helping them onto the back of the creature. A young teenage boy and two elderly women are the next we rescue. Lysander flies them back to the island, leaving them there to wait before we take off for the other three. My heart races when I realise they're far closer to the Charybdis. A child's cry reaches my ears over the storm. "That's a child!"

"What? Where?" Lysander demands, his voice furious. My hand shakes as I point to the boat nearest the monster, slowly being pulled into the current. Lysander turns the creature towards the boat I pointed to, but I see the others. "What about those two over there on the other side? We can't get them both."

Lysander stops the creature near the child's boat. A little girl, no more than three, is crying in a corner, her blonde hair hiding her face. "I'm going to stay with the child," I tell him. "You get the other two on that side. We can't lose any of them, and I'm not leaving that little girl."

"Fucking hell, no." Lysander grits his teeth, looking down at me. "I can't leave you here."

I cup his cheek, speaking into his mind. "I trust you, my enemy. Come back for me." Before he can stop me, I push out of his arms and fling myself off the creature. The wind whips past my face before I hit the water, right next to the boat. I gasp, feeling the current pulling me under as I grab the ropes around the edge of the boat. Lysander's emerald eyes find mine before he speeds off towards the other two. I pull myself into the boat, tripping over a wooden step and landing right in front of the child. She shakes from head to toe in the corner of the boat, and I know this will haunt her for years to come. I'm not so good with children, and I have no idea what to do, but I crawl over to her. Sitting up, I open my arms. "I promise you're safe with me. I'm going to get you out of here."

She lifts her head, her eyes so wide and a bright shade of blue. She throws herself at me, clinging to my neck, and I blow out a breath. The boat rocks and shakes and I pull myself to the edge, looking down at the monster and wishing I didn't. Teeth, millions of yellow, decaying teeth, in a whirlpool of sea water is all I can see for miles. I search the skies for Lysander, finding him by the other boats. Lysander is grabbing the other two as the water starts to speed up around our boat, and we begin to spin. I scream, pulling the girl to me and climbing to the middle of the boat so I don't get thrown out. The girl screams with me, her cries terrible to hear, and I can't do anything.

"I'm here and I'm not letting you get hurt." Lysander's voice roughly fills my mind with a vow from the king of the Water Court to his mate. I look up as Lysander leaves the creature in the air, and he dives straight into the water around the horrifying creature.

"Lysander! What are you—" I pause as water shoots into the air, shaped like a throne, with Lysander sitting right on it. The boat goes still, and I look down to see a cushion of water floating us up into the air. The waters go still around the monster, and it feels like the storms themselves pause for their king.

Lysander stops the sea, stops the waves and the Charybdis. The Charybdis roars, shaking the water with ripples before diving under and leaving the sea still like a lake. Suddenly, Lysander drops down, the golden creature catching him and flying him to us. The boat drops too and crashes into the water. The girl cries, but she is silent as I stand, watching the creature land. Two men help Lysander into the boat, and I put the girl down, handing her to the nobles she must know, and cup his face. He is pale, like he used too much magic, but he is okay. I drop my forehead onto his. "How did you do that?"

"No one has tried to stop him before. To tame these seas. I just did," he answers. I grin just before a portal opens right below the boat, and we crash through it, the boat landing right in front of the empty thrones. Ares and Aphrodite stand in the middle of the empty throne room, with Arden, Emrys and Grayson behind them. I look at them first, wishing they could see me.

Aphrodite looks pleased, and Ares looks murderous. "We will meet you at the Fire Court in three days. Well done, princess. Don't worry, your other loves will be kept close to me."

They leave through a portal, and I reach out for them like there is anything I can do to stop her from taking the rest of my heart with her. Hope clears her throat from the back of the throne room. "We have a problem."

CHAPTER 5

When I was a little girl, I believed that dreams were stories. Stories that you tell yourself in your mind when you're sleeping, and you had complete and utter control over them. I used to dream of pretty unicorns in fields of flowers and fierce dragons burning down castles. I used to dream of seeing my mother smile in the morning, and of times with my father training me in the shadows. I dreamt of the cosy nights in their bedroom, where we'd watch the stars outside the balcony, and they'd tell me about all the constellations while I drank hot chocolate and ate marshmallows that had been roasted over the fires.

But control slips as you age, especially when your life gets drowned in darkness and your dreams turn into nightmares. When the dreams become real things that you can't wake from, no matter how much you try, how much you beg yourself to wake up. But you can't. You're lost, astray within the dream, within the nightmare so real it makes you sweat. It doesn't stop because I want it to; it doesn't disappear even when I beg. I see the commander now, leaning over me, inside his tent that's so dark. His haunting smile, his hands choking me and ripping at my clothes.

I'm powerless to stop the nightmare and powerless to stop him. I can't move, I can't breathe, I can't do anything to stop him. No one's going to stop him. No one's going to help me. I scream and I scream, begging anyone to help, wishing my shadows would help. But no noise leaves my mouth as I scream. Just silence. I can't breathe. I can't do anything. "ELLELIN!"

I hear someone shouting my name. Someone I know. But that can't be right. "Ellelin, you're going to bring the castle down! WAKE UP!" I hear him shouting and shouting, begging for me to wake up, but I'm frozen, looking at the commander leaning over me. He keeps ripping at my clothes, over and over, and—"ELLELIN!"

Gasping, I wake up in a cold room that smells

like salt water, and it's full of shadows. The bed, the castle, is shaking as more and more shadows flood the room, but they don't touch me—but they hurt him. Lysander leans over me, and I scream, backing away from him, crawling up the bed to the headboard of the strange room. It takes me a moment to realise I'm not dreaming, to make the shadows drift away, and to be able to breathe. Water is running around the cuts all over Lysander where my shadows literally were ripping him apart as he tried to wake me. Gods, I didn't mean to do that.

My arms are wrapped tightly around my knees when all my senses fully awaken, and I can see through the fear and know it's Lysander trying to help me. His hands are up at his sides, in surrender, and he is slowly breathing, telling me I'm safe. Waiting for me. His chest is bare, he's wearing nothing but a pair of black shorts, and I can't stop running my eyes over him for a moment. He looks at me, nothing but worry in the depths of his eyes. "It's me. It's only me. I heard you screaming, so I came in. I will not hurt you. I had nightmares too, for years when I was a child. This is the only way my mother could calm me down. She told me repeatedly that I was safe."

"I-I'm s-sorry for hurting you and for the room

I've destroyed," I mutter, flinching at the mess of the room. There are so many cracks in the walls, the floors, and the glass doors to the balcony. Lysander has fully healed himself now. My cloak is still on my shoulders, wrapped tightly around me, and my leather clothes are a sweaty mess. Water cools down my body, and I blink, surprised to realise Lysander is all but washing me with his magic.

"Don't be," he firmly states with all the conviction of a king. "You don't need to tell me what your nightmare is about. I see the same things in my nightmares. I think I'll see the same things until I'm dead."

"I hope I don't. I hope you don't either." My whisper echoes between us. "He doesn't deserve any of us to think about him, even in our nightmares."

We look at each other in the darkness, with only the stars for light, as my breathing calms down. My breath catches and I lower my arms, pulling the blue quilts around me. I don't even remember falling asleep. It's been such a long day since we took back the Water Court. So many were injured already, but as a parting gift, Aphrodite hung up over a thousand nobles outside the castle walls. We saved as many as we could, using my magic and Lysander's to rip down as many of them as possible, who were hanging outside the castle walls above the sea. Alongside any nobles or guards who had the strength to use magic, we saved them. The children were locked away, and thankfully, they didn't hurt them. Lysander and his court are good with healing, but even then, some of the nobles were too far gone. I think the funerals will ring across this court for years.

Hope showed me this spare room only a few hours ago, and I laid down what felt like a minute before I fell asleep. "I came in to check on you earlier, but you were fast asleep. You did a lot for my court today. They are singing your praises and promising you the world."

I sigh. "I did what anyone else would have done."

The silver-touched moonlight shines a glow around Lysander as he gazes out of an arched window that overlooks nothing but stars and seas. "They will never forget, neither will I."

"I'm sorry I couldn't stop the gods sooner," I say quietly before I clear my throat. I'm almost nervous about asking Lysander anything too personal. "What did you used to have nightmares about?"

I see the muscles on his back tense. "About surviving those seas as a child. The creature I tamed...I learned how to tame them pretty quickly when I was down there. I can breathe underwater for longer amounts of time than most of my people, who can just about breathe for ten minutes before their lungs want air, but the cold water used to lock my body up, and I struggled to move. Sometimes I'd just float in the waves for hours, unable to move. I was a child, and my powers weren't what they are now." He looks at me over his shoulder, those startling green eyes locking onto mine. "You could say I dreamt of being powerless and frozen."

In a way, we have the same nightmare. I lift my hand to touch his back before second-guessing myself and lowering it back to the blankets. He carries on talking and I know it's distracting himself more than me. Lysander is the king of denial in every sense. "These golden creatures are kind, easy to tame, and they took me from island to island. I used to pull a fish out of the water to eat, make fires from the trees. Fresh water was more difficult to come by as I had no knowledge of how to get salt out of the salt water. Occasionally, I found islands where the water had been filtered in rivers, but they were few and far between. The islands disappeared at night, and I only allowed myself to sleep for short periods in the day."

"Why didn't you shift into your dragon and just fly away?" I ask, needing to understand him. "Or ask the creature to fly you back home?"

Lysander faces me this time. "It is the way of the kings of the Water Court, and my father was teaching me how to be strong. To leave, to shift, would be a sign of weakness. I am anything but weak."

A protective wave crashes into me, and I blurt out my thoughts without pausing. "I never said you were weak, but I am telling you that your father was wrong to do that, Lysander. You were a child, and it is horrific that you had to endure that. Fuck your father!"

Lysander's smile is cruel, his voice a low whisper. "You would say that. It was your father and your court who killed him."

I blanch, moving backwards, and for a second, he looks like he regretted saying that. Sometimes words cannot be taken back. "I don't know what happened that day, but my father was a good man, and he would have never gotten your father killed for no reason. You forget my father died that day too! If you want to live your life stuck in this state of wanting revenge over everything else, Lysander, then do that, but it won't be with me at your side. There will be nothing between us until you accept the past and stop hiding behind it. You made mistakes, Lysander, but I think deep down you are a good person. Maybe a little fucked up, but at this point, we all are. Stop lying to me, to yourself, to the whole fucking world. You aren't the villain, you aren't my enemy, and until you admit that, then there will be nothing for us."

"Nothing?" He arches an eyebrow, his face full of fury. He crawls over to me, and my eyes widen as he grabs my chin. "There will never be nothing between us, my witch."

Just when I think he is going to kiss me, he pulls back and slides into my bed. "What are you doing? I'm mad at you! Get out!"

He dramatically yawns and it only infuriates me more. "I'm going to sleep, and you are always mad at me. It's a big part of why we are good together."

I push against his shoulder, but he doesn't move. "I did not say you could sleep in my bed! I don't even know your castle, but I'm sure you have other rooms! Go and find one!"

"This room is my new favourite because it smells like you." He pulls the pillow closer and rolls on his side, facing me, all humour gone. "You're still in danger, and I can't sleep without knowing you're safe. Now, I am tired after healing half my court, so we sleep. Tomorrow, we will get my mother and brother back and leave the court to them. We have to save my brothers. For that, we must be rested." He smiles at me as I move to glare at his stupidly perfect face. "Keep glaring at me, witch, and my cock will tell just how much I love that look on your face."

I glare at him with rosy cheeks for another minute, testing my luck, but I know he is right. I slide down the bed and get comfy on my side, facing him. It doesn't take long for Lysander to drift off to sleep, and I roll on my back, looking up at the ceiling for a second before letting my eyes drift once again to him. Lysander's chest is perfect, annoyingly so, and covered in black tattoos or markings, but most are in another language. My skin flushes as I look at him, a dampness growing between my legs. It must be a mate thing, as I can't look at him and not want him. Even when I'm not sure I want that with anyone at the moment. I'm not ready. A symbol for the Water Court is over his heart, a crown wrapped around it, and on his six-pack are more symbols that mean water. I remember them from my childhood lessons from my tutor.

Even with Lysander next to me, my heart is still racing from the nightmare, and every time I close my eyes, I see the commander. Even though I know he's dead, I still feel like what he did has some control over me. It's not fair. He shouldn't have any control over me. Yet here I am, begging my mind to forget, begging my body to let go of the fear it is clinging to. I need air. Throwing the sheets to the side, I rush out to the balcony, closing the glass doors behind me, breathing in the cold, dark and damp air.

This side of the castle is calm, untouched, with nothing but sandy seas for miles. Crystal green seas are so clear that, even in the moonlight, I can see vibrant coral reefs below. The darkness is touched by starlight here, hundreds of stars, and I'm watching them just as a few blink out of existence. My smile is as bright as a star as I feel an all too familiar bond brush against my mind, touching my very soul. Terrin! I watch as the sky is filled with hundreds, if not thousands, of black dragons and a few coloured ones too. Terrin lands on the beach, sending sand flying everywhere. "Are you coming down, princess?"

"This isn't Romeo and Juliet," I joke back to him.

"Who are they?" Terrin asks, completely confused by my joke. Of course, he wouldn't know who they are unless they read Shakespeare in this world. Glancing back at Lysander's room, I smile, knowing he's going to be pissed at me for leaving. He's right, annoying each other is just us. I use my own shadow as shadows to make a small dragon on the edge of the banister before climbing up and sitting down on the dragon. It crashes through the air, landing on the beach and disappearing within a matter of seconds. "Should I be jealous you can make your own dragon and have no need for me now?"

I laugh, shaking my head. "It's not the same. The shadow dragon is powered and controlled by me. Brief trips are fine, but I would struggle to use my powers to both fight and make the dragon to ride."

He rubs his face against my arm. "Fine, I will not be jealous. Much." I look up to see so many hundreds of dragons filling the sky, a few hovering near the castle. "I'm glad that the people of the Water Court got the message from your king not to attack us as we flew in. We passed many of the

Water Court dragons in the skies, and I wouldn't have liked to hurt them to get here."

"You brought all of the Shadow Court with you?" I ask. "There are so many more than I thought."

"They knew their princess was here, fighting, and there is nowhere else we would be. We have our young and eggs with us. We must find safety," Terrin explains to me.

"Go to the Spirit Court island and take it back," I suggest. I wish I could go with him, see my true home once more. I was there for months, clueless that it was my home, the place I was born. Every inch of me longs to be back in the magic castle, to feel the energy of the shadows of the Spirit Court like I did as a child. I just can't return, not yet, but soon. I promise myself soon.

"Leaving you is not something I wish—"

"Terrin, I need you to take back my court and keep my people safe. There's nothing you can do for me here, and I'm not putting you in danger," I firmly state. I run my hand over his scales. "Please. I doubt Ares left the Spirit Court lands without some of his stolen army to watch the castle. I owe you so much for saving me from…"

Terrin growls low, sending shivers down my

spine. "We shall not speak of that monster. He does not deserve to have his name even whispered in our realm."

I clear my throat. "Now that I have my shadow magic back, I wonder if I can do something for you."

"What did you have in mind?" he asks, curious.

"Stay still." I step back, close my eyes, and pull my shadows around him, wrapping tight around every inch of his dragon form and sensing the magic bind that's there around him. It's hard to visualise it, and the magic is incredibly powerful, and I can sense my father all around it. I think he died to make this magic. It feels like chains wrapped around him, and I break them with a lash of my shadows. When I open my eyes, it's not my dragon in front of me anymore. It's a man…a beautiful man. He looks to be a few years older than me, smooth dark skin, a slight dark brown beard that matches his hair, which is long, past his shoulders and silky smooth. His eyes are the exact same as his dragon form, green stars in a dark sky, and he's completely naked. He's gorgeous, but completely and utterly naked. I look up from his body, and he chuckles low, the sound making my skin pebble. I pull off my cloak and drop it between us as I keep my eyes high up. The dragon kings are stunning, the most stunning males I have ever met, and Terrin is right up there with them.

I don't know what they made these dragons with, but fuck, it's dangerous to womankind.

"You can open your eyes now," a dark, deep voice seductively suggests. His voice is darker, different, and I really like it. "I've waited so long to see you as my true self."

He takes a shaky step forward, and I rush over, catching him. "I'd make a *Little Mermaid* reference to getting legs for the first time, but you'd have no idea what I'm talking about." I sigh, reaching up and touching his hair. "I'm not sure how long I can hold the magic back. Whatever my father did, it's so powerful. I'm sorry I can't do more."

Terrin wraps his arms around my waist, and he cups my face with one large hand. There is a ring on his thumb and a symbol I miss seeing. The Spirit Court shadow, with a dragon within the shadow flame. "Mate, if we only have a few seconds, I must taste you."

Terrin kisses me with all the intensity of a burning flame. I gasp at the first taste of him on my lips, a burning attraction coming to life through my chest. He is my mate. It's a different feeling than

Lysander and I have, but so similar, like shadows and light. He might not be good at walking after so many years as a dragon, but kissing? Yup, he has that one down. I lean into him as he breaks away from me, sucking in a deep breath. "Sometimes I imagine the gods never came to our world, and we met in the Spirit Court as teenagers. That we knew from the beginning that we were mates and spent time getting to know each other without war looming over us and magic keeping us apart. I imagine our mating ceremony in front of the courts, of our night in the spirit of darkness underneath the castle where we would be as one for the first time. It is unfair. We never got any of that."

I run my hand down his arm. "And where do Lysander, Arden, Grayson, and Emrys fit into this?"

He laughs and I could listen to him laugh all night. "We would fight to the death for you, and I'd win, of course."

Shaking my head, I laugh at his joke, even if we all do need to talk about this. Somehow, I've ended up in serious relationships with five men, and I don't know how that continues after the war, when the gods are gone and it's just us. Terrin is right in one way. We'd just have the Spirit Court to ourselves, as he is from there. The others have their own courts, and would I be enough for them if I had to go between all of the courts?

"My power is waning," I whisper, pushing my insecure thoughts to the back of my mind. Terrin tucks my hair behind my ear. I sense familiar eyes on us, and I look up to see Lysander on the balcony.

Even with the distance, I feel his burning jealousy and anger like it's my own emotions. "Who the fuck is that?"

"Protect our woman until I am back," Terrin speaks into my mind, but somehow, it's sent to Lysander, too. A shared connection. When I was being attacked by the commander, I thought they spoke through my mind, all of them. How is that possible?

Terrin steps back, dropping my cloak, and I get a glimpse of all of him once again before my spell breaks, his dragon shifting back in a cloud of shadow. "I will wait for you in the Spirit Court, as you wish, and so will your people. Goodbye, my mate. The Spirit Court lands will dampen our bond and speaking to you. However, if you are in danger, I will know still."

He jumps up and flies back into the air, joining the others. With a roar that could shake the very stars, the dragons change direction and head off to our court. "Be safe, Terrin."

I make a dragon out of shadow and fly back up to the balcony, landing in a pit of shadows in front of a very jealous-looking Lysander. He links our fingers. "I don't trust him or like him having you. I don't give a fuck if he is your mate."

"Lysander, I didn't mean to hurt you. Can we all talk—"

"Let's focus on saving the others first, and then we can talk about how you're mine," he coldly answers, leading me back to the bed. Lysander pulls me onto the bed, wrapping his arms tightly around me like I might just disappear into the shadows.

CHAPTER 6

HOPE

The temple of the mighty dragon gods is filled with bodies and mourners. Marble coffins, rows and rows of them, line the temple's stone floor, and the cries of their families echo around like a prayer. Candlelight brightens the dark room, but it does nothing to chase away the grief that is thick in the air. I think they are lucky, the dead and alive in here...they loved someone enough to grieve. People like me...we don't have that. The funerals for the Water Court will go on for weeks, but for now, the bodies are being kept cold by magic. There's a place in Ayiolyn, the Death Mist, where the dead are taken, but for now the priests of the mighty dragon gods, the Twilight themselves, will watch over these lost souls.

I stand in the entrance hall, watching as a family mourns over a coffin, praying for more time that they will not be given. I won't know what it's like to mourn someone like that. The bitter sting of it is hard to swallow at times. I look up at the statues of the gods, sweeping dragons that fill the ceiling, watching over the dead. There are so many forms the dragon gods take. In each court, it is a little different, but this one was always my favourite. Simple dragons, no different to the hundreds of thousands of people around us. The mighty dragon gods have never done anything for me. I'm not sure I even believe in the old stories of them, but the stories stay with me.

I walk outside, done with my work for the morning, my braid hitting my back when the wind blows hard. My boots click on the weathered stone as I head down a pathway that is lined with marble pillars that stretch high up into the arched ceilings. Suddenly, cold water slams straight into me like an arrow, smacking into my back hard enough that I feel my ribs crack. I scream as I cascade through the air, only stopping when my body slams into a pillar and my head smacks hard against the stone. Dizziness heavily weighs me down as I try to rise to my feet, leaning against the pillar and wheezing.

My eyes widen in fear as ice freezes around my body, locking me in place and making it impossible to move. My fingers stretch for my dagger at my side, reaching for anything to save myself, but they freeze too until I can't feel anything through the bitter cold. Just as the ice is crawling up my neck, a tall man steps out in front of me. A noble of the Water Court, if I had to guess from his expensive clothes and perfect dark skin. His black hair is in dreadlocks, falling around his face and dripping with water. Blue magic swirls around his hand, and his eyes match the colour of his power. I don't know him, and I don't have any idea why he's attacking me. "Why?" I manage to croak out, clawing at the ice at my side with my nails. It spreads around my body, tight and strong, and fear makes me panic.

If someone doesn't come soon, no one is going to come to save me. I don't have anyone. There's no one here that even likes me in this court, even if I care about some of the people I grew up around. I don't have a family; I have no one looking after me. Nothing. It would be a while before anyone even noticed I was gone. Lysander's mother might have looked for me, but she is wallowing in her rooms, thick in grief and sadness for those lost. "You're the king's mistress, or whatever they want to call you. Many of us are not in fact happy with him and his rule. He got my wife killed!"

"Not my problem, you fucking psychopath!" I snarl. "Killing me won't get her back or even bother Lysander! You fool!"

Rage fuels him, and my words don't help. Fuck, I'm so screwed. "She was slaughtered by that goddess, all because she decided to be loyal to King Lysander. I don't know why she thought that was a good idea. He is not a king worth being loyal to. So, I thought I'd take what was his. He clearly likes you, kept you around, it's well known within the court. I'm sorry."

"Stop!" I shout at him, begging. I don't beg for anyone, but for my life…I'll beg right now for my life. The ice starts covering my mouth, like he can't stand to listen to me. No, he wants to drown me. Water sharply pours down my throat, and I gasp, only making it worse as it suffocates me. I struggle against the ice holding me, choking on the water, and the man smirks, pure vengeance glistening in his eyes. Never in my life have I wanted to be something more than mortal.

Someone save me.

Please, someone.

As darkness begins to shadow my vision, I try not to close my eyes, to give up. Just when I think it's over, that my life is done for, glowing green water wraps around the man, picking him up and slamming him upon the wall hard enough to make it crack. His power breaks on me, only enough that I can just about breathe through the thin ice. Xandry steps out of the shadows of the pillars, a black cloak falling off his shoulders, matching the darkness of his soft hair that is lacking the gel he usually uses to style it. I prefer it like this, natural and soft. Xandry, my childhood friend and former tutor, just saved my life.

Damning fury is written over his face, from his blazing red eyes to the tight line of his lips as he heads towards the man. In two steps, he is in front of the man, and he uses his power far better, far quicker than I knew possible. Xandry makes a dagger out of ice and sends it spiralling straight into his throat, locking him in place on the wall as the life drains from his eyes. Xandry wraps his hand around the hilt, pushing in further. Hot red blood pours in rivers down the man's body and over Xandry's hands before he lets go and leaves him there.

My heart is racing as Xandry turns to me, anger

fading to pure concern. The ice finally starts to snap under his power, breaking around me till I fall straight to the floor, coughing and spluttering in pain. He picks me up, setting me on the ground, and his magic washes over my body, healing my ribs and the lump on my head in moments. "Hope, can you breathe for me? He's dead and you are safe."

"Safe?" I humourlessly laugh, pushing him off me. I breathlessly drop onto the stone step next to him, ignoring the look he gives me. I need a minute. I focus on the palm trees blowing in the breeze near us, the sparkling clear sand, the sound of the wind blowing through the air. "Don't be patronising." I look at the man behind, blood pouring into the water. I am surprised he thought it was a good idea to attack anybody in this court. He would have died for it either way. Maybe he just wanted to be with his wife and was happy to die taking me with him. I look at Xandry. "What are you doing here? You were at the spirit castle, tutor."

He ignores my sarcasm. "The castle saved me, showing me out through a portal to this court. To home."

"Lucky you. I got thrown headfirst into a desert," I snap. Somehow, he made it out better than anyone. Typical Xandry. I stand up, not wanting to be around him any longer than I need to be. "I didn't know that you were allowed to kill people in your religion. What will the Twilight say?"

He rises to his feet, towering over me. "We're allowed to protect ourselves against attacks."

"He was hardly attacking you." I lift my chin, calling him on his bullshit.

He leans into my space, and I can't help but notice how much Xandry has grown. The gangly boy has turned into a man, a thickly muscled man who is stunning. "You could just say thank you, Hope. Or have you never said those words before?" He steps further into my space, pushing me against the pillar so that I can't escape him. "Here, I'll teach you. *Thank you*," he says, enunciating them slowly. "Two words, usually you feel gratitude with them."

"Fuck you," I snarl. I should push him away.

He grins, and it takes my breath away. "Why didn't you fight him off? The Hope I knew was quicker than that asshole."

I grit my teeth. "He surprised me. I was thinking of something else, and he got lucky."

"Our old tutor would be pissed to see you today. Come and train with me in the mornings," he asks.

"Let me help you. We grew up in this court together, after all." He looks into my eyes. "You can fight better than that. You know better than that, Hope."

"And I made a mistake," I all but shout at him. "Just stop it. I'm not training with you." I hate that he's bringing our past up, like I owe him anything. In truth, there was a moment where I liked him. He's right, we did train together as kids. There was a group of twenty of us at the beginning, but most dropped out until there were just five left. All of us are orphans, parentless wards within the courts. I don't know what happened to his parents. I never asked, but he was in the Water Court with me for years. We were the top of the class, always neck and neck in our battles. I was obsessed with Lysander even at a young age, but Xandry… I didn't know it then, but he became my best friend for a while.

Then the asshole decided, out of the blue, that he didn't want to be anything to anybody and chose the mighty gods. He chose to be a priest over being my friend. You can't have a best friend, not when he serves the gods, and he left without a goodbye. For some reason, even back then, it upset me as much as it does to this day. I push away from the wall, shoving at his arm, and he clearly lets me go. I start walking away from him, and he catches up to my side. "I should walk you back to your room to continue to see that you are well."

A woman's scream of horror echoes out of the space behind us. "You just left a dead body pinned to the wall. You probably should go back there and sort that."

Xandry waves a hand. "They have seen plenty of dead. I am sure another priest will come and sort out the body."

I shake my head at him. "You have answers for everything, but not one truth. Why did you leave the training and go to the gods without saying a word to me?" I turn on him as the words blurt out.

To my horror and embarrassment, he says nothing. Nothing for so long that it hurts to breathe. Coward. I turn away from him, my cheeks burning, and leave. He carries on walking with me and changes the subject, like the last few moments were nothing. "Where have you been?"

Small talk, really? I sigh. "With the princess of the Spirit Court and learning to be a dragon rider."

I swear there is pride in his eyes. "You have a dragon?"

"Yes." I touch my chest, feeling that bond even now, to the dragon that I miss dearly. Maybe she can feel me calling for her. Maybe she will come to me one day, maybe she won't. It makes me sad to think that she won't come this far. She is a wild dragon, after all, with deep ties to the West. I do sense her close, closer than before, but she hasn't come for me.

Xandry touches my arm, stopping me from running away, and all I can focus on is his hand against my bare skin, the burn of his touch. "I heard male priests aren't allowed to touch females unless they are healing them."

He doesn't remove his hand. "Breaking the rules seems to be a theme for you and me today."

My heart pats hard in my chest, surprising me. I haven't felt anything like this before. "Hope, you should make sure Lysander looks after you better. Armed guards or some shit a king can order. Letting you be attacked like that is not fitting for a future queen."

I blink. "Lysander has nothing to do with me anymore. We're not together."

Pure surprise laces his eyes, but he doesn't say anything. He never says anything. Xandry drops his hand from my arm, and he walks away from me, like he did all those years ago. Yet I still feel as bitterly angry as I did back then, maybe even worse. Why does everyone walk away from me like I mean nothing?

CHAPTER 7

I don't know what exactly I expected from the Fire Court, but walking in, it's like being in a sauna. It's boiling hot, like walking into a desert where it never rains and the heat threatens to engulf you with every breath. I instantly regret wearing tight, armoured leather trousers and a black top with long sleeves. The Water Court symbol is all over my clothes, and I feel very out of place in the Fire Court all of a sudden. At least my hair is up and off my neck, where a sweat is already building up. The high ponytail moves with my every step, the end of the braid hitting the small of my back.

The Fire Court smells like ash, blood, and wine. I glance at Lysander at my side, who looks a thousand times better than he did in the test. Now he is back wearing his usual tight-fighting clothes, and his blue crown is nestled in his thick red hair, which he has cut shorter. A blue sword is on his back, one I've not seen before, but his expression is familiar. There is a look of pure and utter vengeance on his face as he holds my hand as we walk down the long room towards the fire throne.

The fire throne room itself is simpler than I would've expected Arden's throne room to be, but there is blood all over the black tiles, mixed in with the flame outlines. A giant stained glass flame is behind two simple seats with an entire domed window room at the back, again filled with stained glass, all brilliant and vibrant reds. It makes the entire room glow in an eerie red-orange haze.

There are benches, rows of them on either side of the pathway, filled with the Fire Court people. They are dressed smarter than us, in short red tube tops and long red skirts, and the men are in dark red shirts and matching shorts. The Fire Court nobles at the front look terrible, and most of them are crying. There are no children here again, and I wonder where they locked them up this time. In front of the Fire Court people are dozens of enchanted guards, clarifying that the people can't escape even if they tried.

I look around them for just a moment. My eyes flicker across each of them, seeing the same desperation, panic in their eyes. The same shared wish that they weren't here, that anything else was happening, and they watch me with a mixture of curiosity and hope. Pulling my gaze forward, I try not to focus on their looks of hope that seem like stars in a dark sky. I might not be able to help them, because I made a deal with the gods for the men I love, and I could have cursed everyone in this world by doing so. I refuse to let my head drop when I see my dragon kings, even if my heart feels like it's left my chest and is in my stomach now.

I remind myself I've done something good with Lysander, at least. The Water Court is safe, and I saw my family only this morning before we left for the Fire Court, two days earlier than Aphrodite demanded we come. I briefly saw my mother and grandmother, only for a moment, while Lysander's mother and brother came back to the court. My grandmother has had no luck waking my mother up. She's just as still and just as peaceful as she was before. Livia has gone home, Arty and Hope are safe in the Water Court, and for a moment, I felt like

I might actually be able to do this. That was until I came here. I need to ask Ares exactly what he's done to my mother. He must be aware by now that I've taken her.

The Fire Court is so much different from my memories as a child, running about with Arden. Neither of us knew, the next time I'd come here, he would be a prisoner and I would be fighting for him. He was just the annoying boy I didn't much like as a child, and now he is everything I want. Everything I need. Ares and Aphrodite are seated on the thrones, on plush red cushioned seats, leaning away from the open pools of lava on either side of the thrones, which are spitting up embers now and then. Aphrodite has a different red dress on now; this one is full of gemstones in a corset and a short miniskirt.

"You're early." Her melodic voice rings out. She stands up when we stop, and walks to Arden. My hands tighten when she makes him stand, and she leans into him, pushing her entire body against his. She runs her hands up his arms, and I take a step forward, shadows pooling at my feet. I'm going to fucking kill her for touching him. Lysander grabs my arm, pulling me to his side. "He would never want her. Trust me, I would know, considering how much he fucking loves you is a constant annoyance to me. It's the spell, not him. She is teasing you into attacking and giving her a reason to hurt him."

I try to listen to Lysander's warning, but I feel like I can't breathe until she finally leans back, sighing and walking back to the throne. Arden takes several steps toward us before dropping on his knees in front of the thrones, that red haze all over his eyes. He looks thinner than before, but there seems to be no new bruises, no fresh blood. Emrys and Grayson are so still, the red tint of magic glowing in their eyes, and it takes more strength than I thought I had not to go to them, shake them, and beg them to snap out of it. "We're here for your test. Didn't want to leave my friend's court in your lovely hands for too long."

Arden looks straight through me like I'm not here—like nothing's here, for that matter. I try very hard to pull my eyes up to meet Aphrodite's. She grins before winking once. "I don't feel like having a long conversation with you today. I'm tired. It was a long night with the company of the Fire Court. They sure do know how to throw a party."

Ares looks bored, running his hand over his staff. He really loves that thing. "Just get straight to the test. It will be more entertaining than listening to her rant on." He meets my gaze for a second.

I smirk. "I agree, I want to get back to my family." His eyes turn into slits full of indignation.

Aphrodite raises her hand, a portal opening to our left. She looks far too confident. "Go on, lovebirds." She clicks her fingers at Arden, and he rises to his feet like her puppet. I grit my teeth, trying not to say anything. Lysander is still, but I can feel the fury rolling off him. I wonder if our mating bond makes him feel my emotions too, how livid I am, until it becomes a part of his own emotions.

Arden moves like a robot to the portal. Each step is absolutely controlled, and I watch the man I love with a desperation fuelled in my heart. Arden's muscular body moves tensely, like he is fighting back against the hold, and I can't do anything but watch this beautiful man. His shoulder-length dark hair is wavy, and it only highlights his perfect jawline, high cheekbones and how stunning he is. He takes my breath away, and I know I could stare at him forever, always finding something new to admire.

He walks through the portal, to the other side, which is all red from what I can see. Aphrodite's words from the beginning of the test come back to me. She spoke, "*In the court of Fire, flames burn away any lies.*"

What does that mean? Lysander tugs me with him through the portal, and it snaps shut behind us. The blistering, sweltering heat sticks to me here, far worse than the Fire Court, and my throat feels like it's burning with each breath. We're on a rock in the middle of the volcano, lava in every direction around us, and I can barely see the edges of the volcano we are standing within. The ground gently shakes, loose pebbles tapping on the rock, by my feet.

"You're here, princess."

Arden. My gaze fixes on him as he stares back at me, and his eyes don't have that red haze anymore. My feet are moving before my mind has caught up, and I close the space between us, throwing my arms around his neck, squeezing him tight. "You're okay. You're really okay."

He cups my face, running his eyes over me. "What are you doing here, and why are you not on Earth?"

I lean back, out of his touch. "We can have a long discussion later about the fact that you decided it was a great idea to leave me on Earth after everything that happened. I've already told Lysander how much of a royally fucked-up idea that was, and I am so, so furious with you all. I thought…" I pause, my heart racing. "I thought we were in this together. If you fall, if Ayiolyn falls, I will be at your side and nowhere else. How dare you decide if I want to be here or not."

"We decided because we love you and know you. You'd fight, with every breath you have, and die. You had no powers, princess, and—"

I fling my arms out. "There is being protective and there is crushing someone's soul in the name of protecting them."

Lysander moves to my side. He looks uncomfortable. "We will have this discussion later, but not when we are in a test and close to burning in lava." He looks at the lava with pure disgust, like it's the most horrid thing he has ever seen. Water king through and through.

I cross my arms, frustration bubbling in my chest. "I'm not discussing it repeatedly. When all four of you are together, we'll discuss everything."

Arden strokes his hand down my arm before taking my hand and linking our fingers. "I'm sorry."

Lysander is right. We need to focus. Arden might look at home in this volcano, but the rest of us are not comfortable here. "Where are we?"

Arden grins and it makes me smile for a moment, remembering my funny, flirty fire king. "This is in the centre of my court. We're not in any danger here. The fires will not burn you as long as you're telling the whole truth. I don't understand why Aphrodite brought us here for entertainment or a test at all. We can just walk to the portal and get out." He points to a small ledge in the distance, where there is a portal and a lot of lava between us. "There needs to be no major secrets between us, which I doubt there is, to escape. We'll be able to simply walk out of here as long as we are truthful. My father used to bring traitors here to get them to tell the truth about crimes, or they'd just stay here forever if they decided not to and die eventually from the lava." He grins at me. "I've never seen or heard of that happening. Most people tell the truth because they want to get out. My father would usually show them mercy, unless they were traitors to the throne."

Lysander looks at me, and my blood feels like it's on fire, matching the lava. Arden is oblivious, a trait that is going to cause us problems. Aphrodite put us here because she must have known about Lysander and me. About the blackmail. If we tell Arden right now, he might not forgive us. "But there's no major secrets between us three, is there? We know everything, so we can simply—"

Arden goes to step on the lava, and I roughly grab his arm to stop him. Confusion is written all over his handsome face as he steps back. Confusion is better than pain, which is what he is going to feel soon. Lysander is watching me. "Are you going to tell him, or am I going to? I don't feel like letting him get burned to death to keep this secret."

Lysander runs his hand through his hair, roaring to the dark skies above us. "How the fuck did she know?"

Arden lets my hand go, looking between us now, and the distrust in his eyes cuts through my chest. Oh god, he is going to hate me. He walks to Lysander, grabbing his shirt. "What did she know? The truth, now!"

Lysander pushes him away, and he doesn't say anything for such a long time. I know I need to tell him. I clear my throat, and they both look at me. I focus on Arden, on Arden who is amazing and doesn't deserve this. "When I first came back to Ayiolyn for the Dragon Crown Race—"

"I'll tell him," Lysander interrupts me. "It wasn't all you."

"But I'm the one in love with him, so it should

come from me." I turn to Arden, hating the betrayal written all over his face and he doesn't even know yet. My stomach drops as I make the words leave my mouth. "When I was put into the crown test, do you remember I didn't like you at the beginning? I didn't want to get close to you because you killed my ex-boyfriend."

Arden's voice is bitter. "He deserved it."

"Not the point," I whisper, feeling my eyes filling with tears for the dragon who killed my ex when we met, but he did it to save me. For the king I never meant to betray…but I did.

Arden rubs his chin. "I don't get why we're talking about the past. What happened back then is not a secret."

I look once more at Lysander before making sure to focus on Arden as I tell him everything. "On that first night, Lysander cornered me in the bathroom. He made it very clear that if I didn't do what he wanted, he was going to kill my grandmother."

Arden rounds on Lysander. "You sick bastard, why would you do that? She was a terrified mortal, who we kidnapped. Why would you scare her? What could have been worth it?" Arden looks at me. "What did he ask you to do?"

Clearing my throat, I answer him. "He blackmailed me, told me to get close to you, to make you fall in love with me. Then he was going to get me to kill you because it would hurt you more to have someone you love kill you. Some of the times when I agreed to walk with you, to talk with you, some of it was because I was scared of what Lysander would do to me. What he would do to my grandmother if I didn't at least appear like I was trying to get close to you." His heart breaks in front of me. Tears roll down my cheeks as I reach for him, but he steps back. "But it became real. It became real so quickly, because I couldn't shake the feeling that I knew you and trusted you. It annoyed me because I don't trust anybody and there was so much risk in loving you. It was real, it is real."

Arden huffs a laugh, but he doesn't interrupt me. "I knew when you kissed me. Remember that time that you kissed me in your room after giving me the ring? Lysander was there, and he made an ice dagger in my hand. He made it very clear that he believed that you were already in love with me at that point, but I couldn't do it. I could not do it, even when I knew what could happen, even if there was a good chance that he'd go and kill my grandmother. My *only* family left. I could not do it, so I sacrificed everything for you. Please don't hate me for this, because I do love you, but that's the truth. The truth between us that she dropped us here for."

Arden is still. "Quiet, princess."

Lysander looks at Arden, no apology in his eyes. Just nothing but the cold mask he wears. "We need to talk alone," my fire king says with ice in his gaze.

I raise my eyebrows at Arden's request. "I'm not leaving you two alone right now." Neither of them looks away from each other, like wolves preparing to fight. "I'm going to be right here, in the middle of you both, where I've been permanently since the minute I came back to this world. It seems like we were always heading for this, and if you fight now, if you kill each other, then the only person who wins is Aphrodite. Your courts need you…I need you. I'm not okay, I'm trying, but I am not okay, and if you destroy each other, then I lose everything. You'd only be hurting me and your courts."

Arden meets my eyes for a second, his gaze softening, but then he turns back to Lysander with a vengeance. "Why?"

"Your father, for what he did. He got mine killed," Lysander answers, simple and straight to the point. But it's like looking at a bomb covered in thick ice, cracking every so often, and soon it will explode, taking everything with it. "That's what I believed at the time. I thought it was your father that took mine to the Spirit Court, but it wasn't just him to blame. I didn't think there was anyone left in the Spirit Court, but everyone who is to blame for my father's death is on this rock."

"You did this for your father? You betrayed me, a fucking brother to you, for him?" Arden shouts. "Your father was a monster!"

"Shut the fuck up!" Lysander shouts.

"Do you think you're the only court that whispers? Just because your mum lived in a delusional world and thought he was a good person, it doesn't mean he was." Lysander goes very still. I can practically taste the fury burning between them, the anger.

"Guys, it's not…"

Lysander steps into Arden's face. Arden doesn't budge, even a step. "You know nothing about my father!"

"I know everything. So did everyone else, except you, it seems. We never spoke about it, but I was sure you knew. I was sure you wanted to be better than him, a good fucking person. The Water Court wasn't a good place when your father ruled.

He was cruel, malicious, and death was a game to him. The royalty test was something sick he came up with. Nobody else had done it before you. He didn't do it as a child. That was a test he invented for you because he was adamant that his sons needed to be strong. Did you know you had a sister? Older than you that died in that test? I heard my mother talking with yours about how your father had taken everyone's memories of the firstborn princess, even yours. She asked my mother if it was possible for those memories to be given back, but it's not."

Lysander shakes his head. "You're lying."

"Lies are part of you and your family, but I hoped you were better. Ask your mother, fuck, even your brother. Everyone knew but treated you like the unstable fucker you are and never said a word."

Lysander is shaking with fury, but Arden keeps pushing. "You don't think my father would have asked your father for help unless there was a dire need for it? Your father never helped, never did anything to try to save anyone. Probably the only good thing that your father ever did in his entire life was go to the Spirit Court and try to save everybody. You're angry about the only good thing that he did in his entire rule. You're angry for fucking nothing!" Arden grabs his shirt, pulling him closer. "You're my brother, not in blood but in my heart, and you've fucking cut it out and destroyed it. I chose you, broken and all, as my family, and you blackmailed the girl I love, tried to kill me, and betrayed everything good you had. You're on your fucking own from now on!"

My heart cracks, and I realise it's Lysander's pain I'm feeling too. He is destroyed by this too. How can we get past this?

"I don't need you." Lysander pushes him away.

"But you need her, don't you?" Arden asks, waving a hand at me. "You blackmailed her when she was fucking terrified, and now she's your destined mate. Isn't there an irony in that? Someone that you broke, scared, and used to get close to your enemy actually ended up falling in love with your enemy. You were right to tell her to kill me then. I was already in love with her from the moment I met her."

"Stop. Please." I step up next to them both. "You're family. Please, we can fix this. I know you loved your father, Lysander. It's okay to love him and agree that he wasn't a good person. But you need to stop this revenge, stop hating everybody. I'm on Arden's side with this. You need to put it behind you if we have any chance of a future."

"He's not going to do that, princess. I don't think he is even capable of doing the work to be a good person."

That's the final straw for Lysander, and he slams a spear of water straight at Arden's chest, but that's a mistake. Arden catches it, and it turns into mist. Arden is in his element, in every sense of the word, and the fire here is fuel. I rush away from them both as streams of lava explode out of the volcano, heading right for Lysander. He defends himself with water from the very sky, and they meet in a clash of deadly steam, as I scream and duck. It doesn't touch me, as though they have willed it not to. Sobbing, I watch them fight, knowing this is my fault. I scream, begging them to stop, but they don't.

Eventually everything seems to fade, and I find Arden holding Lysander down on the ground, his face inches from lava. It is burning his arm as he screams and roars underneath him, and I feel my arm heating like I can feel his burning, too. Arden punches Lysander hard in the face. "How the fuck could you do that to me? I was there for you." He punches him again. Lysander isn't fighting him.

Why isn't he fighting back? "I was there again and again for you, and you were fucking betraying me!"

He punches him one more time as I run over and grab his arm. Arden looks at me. "Please stop. He's my destined mate. Please, for me, stop."

Arden pushes off my hand and rises off Lysander. "For her. You fucking worthless asshole."

He walks across the lava, leaving us both behind. Lysander is a bloody mess, matching my heart as it cracks to splinters. We might have won the test, but Aphrodite definitely did better. I glance at my hand, at the mark there and see the fire chain is gone, along with the water one. I shake my head at Lysander before stepping onto the lava after Arden, heading back to the Fire Court. As I walk across the lava, it's only then that I feel it. Arden, in my mind, and his emotions like a fiery, angry vortex.

A mate bond.

Arden is my destined mate, and he hates me.

CHAPTER 8

ARTEMIS

"You could have sent her body to the Mist. To be buried with our people."

I barely move when Prince Kian steps to my side, his words barely an echo to my ears as I picture the woman who cared for me my entire life being killed. Again. I see her in my nightmares, in daydreams…whenever I close my eyes. I was powerless, weak, and useless to stop my mother from murdering her. I tuck my wavy locks behind my ear.

"She did not want that." I keep my voice quiet, like the dead need my whispers, and I never look away from my nanny's grave. The grave is simple yet elegant, her body laid within the earth, a headstone with small water droplets from the rain running down it. Her name etched in the stone for time to keep. There are water lilies spread across the small circular pond above her grave. Her favourite flowers. I used to get them for her as a child because I loved how she smiled at me. I blow out a breath, trying to force myself to talk about her like it doesn't gut me. "She was from Earth and spoke often about wanting to go back. Tara told me once, when she died, to bury her body in the ground, with water lilies above. Beauty hiding away death, she said."

He touches my hand with his, warmth spreading between us. The handsome prince meets my eyes with his green emeralds, his so bright and full of hope. Prince Kian's scent reminds me of raindrops, but musky and dark, and I breathe it in. I love how it wraps around me, protecting me, settling my nerves. I don't deserve to feel safe around him. I don't deserve his friendship, either. The prince of the Water Court looks down at the grave of a woman he didn't know yet helped make possible. Kian found this small green garden, hidden in the castle, and he gave it to me to make her grave.

When he came back with his mother, he found me alone with her body, crying so hard the blood vessels in my eyes burst. I didn't want to move. I wanted to die with her at that moment. Kian was the one who picked me up off the floor, helped me heal, and gave me strength. He carried her body to the temple for the priests to wrap her, and then he helped me dig this grave. I wanted to dig it on my own, but he stayed. He helped me find the flowers, and he made the pond with his magic so the water will never change. The headstone was from him; he ordered it, and it was delivered the next morning. I guess there are perks to being a prince.

I'm glad he likes me, if I'm being honest. He's the only one in the Water Court who does. I don't know where I'm going to go next. Staying in the Water Court can't be a permanent solution to my life, but…I don't think I'm safe anywhere else.

"Arty, tell me what's going on in your mind." I turn to him, my eyes filled with tears that I won't let fall. He never falters as he looks at me. "I can't help you if you don't talk to me."

"And why do you want to help me?" I softly ask. "You don't owe me anything. I know you might feel that way because I got you out of the prisons, but you don't."

"Arty," he breathes my name gently. Like my name holds a million secrets between us. He runs a hand through his short red locks of hair, his jaw tightening. "That's not—"

"All of your people hate me because of what my parents did, and you should be one of them. I'm not good, not like you." My words are bitter, sharp. "Some might think if you spend time with me, you might end up just as terrible."

"You're not them," he firmly replies. "And if you are terrible, then so am I." He's shaking his head at me as he steps closer. I can barely breathe when he's this close, when his body's pressed against mine, and when there's nothing between us. This, this is what it's like to fall in love. I know it, and it's terrifying. I will ruin him. "Come, let's go and walk down by the beach. I know it's your favourite place. The sun will be setting soon, and it will be quiet. We can talk more."

He offers me his arm and I sigh. "You're like a valiant prince from a fairy tale. Endlessly trying to save the day."

Kian's laugh vibrates around me as I take his arm. "I'll take that. I am a prince, and saving you is something I'm invested in. Even from yourself."

I lower my head, looking away. Looking at him for too long is dangerous, and listening to him is too.

Sometimes, he makes me dream of a wonderful future, of peace and happiness, things I have never once thought I would be allowed to have. Because he's right, hurting myself with insults is normal. Whispers follow us as we walk through the court, through the long corridors and the sweeping pathways that lead out to the beach at nearly every edge of the castle.

The whispers haunt me, echoing so loud they chase at my feet like mice: *she shouldn't be here; why has our king not killed her; they should use the girl to get back at her parents; she's evil; she should not be in our court.*" So many whispers, so many death threats…it doesn't stop here. Prince Kian keeps his head high throughout it, like he can't hear them, like their whispers aren't real. I wish I could do that, but I can't. Each whisper is pounding into my head with every moment, making my heart leach of colour.

Kian sighs when we are out of the castle, patting my hand. "My people are stubborn, but give them time and they will give you a chance. A real chance."

"I don't think they will ever give me a chance. They will ever only see me as the person who is the daughter of them, who betrayed your king, essentially," I remind him.

"You have a choice in everything, and we are not our parents," he reminds me. "If they knew you like I did, they'd know that you did not have a choice back then and you're trying to make it better. We all make mistakes. Trying to fix them is what makes us better people." I don't answer him about that. Mostly because I don't know what to say to him. Can you ever be forgiven for what you've done? I killed people, innocent people. I lied to and betrayed someone who's my friend. I let *him* out, my father calling back my mother with him. The pair of them are lashing out havoc on the world as only gods can do. I might not be my parents, but I'm as terrible as they are with my past actions.

We stroll along the beach for a while, and Kian is right about one thing. The gentle beach here is one of my favourite places. The golden sands, the crystal green water, and the peace here lures me in. The sun shines down brightly on us as we walk, and people at the court are in the water themselves, playing, swimming, ignoring us while they enjoy their families. I suck in a breath of the salty air as we walk until it's just me and him on an empty beach. I can finally breathe a little without the prying eyes of the court. "Arty, can you—"

"Help!" a panicked young voice screams. We

both stop, looking around, but there's nothing but sandy beaches, a few palm trees, and the sea. That's it. I hear the splashing first before Kian sharply looks across the water. He lets go of my hand, and in seconds he's running, jumping into the sea, the water moving around him, almost propelling him through the green, almost blue waves. He is so fast in the water, the water prince indeed, and he heads right towards the small dot of what I think is a floating child. Kian swims faster and faster before diving under, and for seconds, there is nothing but the waves brushing against my feet, my heart pounding in my chest. I ready myself to swim in after them, having no idea if I can move fast enough to even help them.

I watch the shoreline like time itself has stood still, until quickly Kian breaks out of the water nearby, holding a boy that can be only about eight or nine. Water pours off them both, and the boy is floppy, hanging off Kian's arms. He is completely unconscious...maybe not even breathing. Kian carefully drops him on the beach next to me and puts his fingers on his neck to check his pulse. "He's not breathing. Fuck."

The pale, blond-haired boy is very still as my

hand cups my mouth. "Oh god. Do something, Kian!"

Kian places his hands over the boy's chest and closes his eyes. Powerful blue healing magic swirls around him and the boy, water pouring out of his hands and from the very sea behind him, covering the boy from head to toe except for his mouth and nose, willing him to breathe.

This has to work. Kian is a powerful healer. He can—"I'm not strong enough to start his heart again. He's been out too long. I'm not my brother."

Kian doesn't give up, even when he sounds defeated. My heart races as I look down at the boy, and I reach over and put my hand on Kian's shoulder to comfort him, tears falling down my face. Suddenly his magic amplifies, exploding out of him, rays of blue light shining in every direction. The boy gasps, coughing, choking on air in the middle of us, and Kian's magic snaps away like a switch just turned off.

I quickly turn the boy onto his side, patting his back firmly as he coughs out water for a good few minutes, my heart racing with him. When he stops, we both help the boy sit up. Kian looks right at me in shock. "How did you do that, Arty? I've never felt anything so strong, not even from Lysander…"

"I-I didn't do anything," I splutter, shaking my head. "I don't even understand how this happened. It was your power."

"It was mine but—" Kian is cut off by the sound of a woman shouting. We both look over to see a woman in a silver dress rushing down the beach towards us. No, towards the boy. She flings herself at the boy, pulling him on her lap and kissing his head. Kian softly tells her what happened, finishing with a suggestion to see the healers just in case.

"Thank you," the woman cries, cupping her son's face. "What are you doing here? You ran off." She's obviously not from the Water Court. I would guess Air Court from just the look of her and the silver clothes she wears.

The boy hiccups. "I wanted to see the sea, and then I was paddling, but it pulled me in. I was scared…"

"Are you from the Air Court?" Kian asks. "I heard refugees had been taken in yesterday."

"Oh, you're the prince!" the woman exclaims. "And yes, we are."

Kian looks at the shocked boy. "You should be careful near the oceans. The sea is alive and playful. It pulls you in, thinking you are a Water Court child who can breathe underwater. It didn't mean to hurt you." The boy nods, looking fearfully at the water. "Why don't I teach you how to swim another time? It is safe, with the right tips."

"I'd like that." The boy nods and his mother smiles brightly at them.

After many more thanks and expressions of her gratitude, she leaves us, and I lie back on the sand. Kian lies next to me. "Do you really not know what happened there? It was likely all your power."

Kian takes my hand, linking our fingers. "It wasn't my power. You're the child of two gods, Artemis. You've been told that you're powerless your entire life, but you did something then. One day, your power is going to break free, and I will be here for you when it does."

I don't know what I did to deserve Kian. "I was born powerless; that doesn't just change."

He tightens his grip on my hand. "Something has changed. Everything can change. You are not powerless."

Maybe he is right.

CHAPTER 9

The Fire Court walls look like amber, like they're glowing alive with real flames instead of crystals. The crystals are designed within the very walls themselves, like the fire dragons flying outside the castle built the walls, the archways, and amber doors from the flames of their mouths. I run my hand against the smooth, cool amber walls, seeing the light making the crystals dance within it. It's beautiful, unlike my dreams, unlike my reality. Everything is broken, including me. I couldn't sleep, not for a moment. This time, my nightmare is not just about the commander, it's about Arden and Lysander too. The hate that has built in them has exploded into this living thing between the three of us. I can't fix them, I wouldn't know how to start, and sometimes I feel like I'm going to burn trying to get close.

The Fire Court is now safe from Ares and Aphrodite, back in the hands of their king, who they openly adore. It turns out most of the Fire Court hid, protected by deadly fires that the gods couldn't slip through. However, there were many, many deaths of nobles who chose to stay to keep the gods busy and their families safe. Their bodies are being looked after by the Twilight for now. I'm a stranger here, but I like how loyal they are to Arden. No one in this court was under Aphrodite's magic; they were too strong willed. The Fire Court lost a few hundred people, including important nobles, but the majority of the Fire Court was safe. It was apparently hard for the gods to invade, to get into the court, and they didn't have enough time here to do much in the way of ruling.

They were gone when we came back, and part of me wishes they weren't—just so I could see Emrys and Grayson one more time. I feel like I'm living for seconds with them, moments where they don't even know me. I don't even know which court they've gone to next, but I hope Arden or Lysander have sent out spies to find out. I don't think Lysander's in the castle anymore. I didn't look or even dare ask Arden, who was silent at my side, but I can feel Lysander's not close. Arden is close, his emotions like a firestorm. I search for him in the castle, knowing I want to see him, even if he doesn't want to see me right now. Sleeping is not happening either way.

"What are you doing out here alone? You're in constant danger, and you should have guards. Where is Arden?" Hope demands, making me jump. I turn to see her storming down the corridor to me, like a wolf that's found her prey. She looks at my face, and her expression morphs from anger to concern. I don't want her concern. "You should be sleeping."

Crossing my arms, I turn away from her and carry on walking. "No, I shouldn't. I also don't need guards. I have my powers. Today's test wasn't exactly hard work, so I'm fine." I want to add that I don't sleep much anymore these days, but I don't. I hold that truth close to my chest, including how I slept for the first time when I had Lysander there and actually felt safe. "What are you doing in this court?"

"I came through the portal a few hours ago, from the Water Court, to see how things were going. Lysander is there, and I thought it was weird you weren't with him," she prods. "He also looked ready to drown his kingdom. What happened today?"

"You probably should stay in the Water Court. Drowning is easier than burning, so I've heard," I mutter.

She raises an eyebrow. "Come on, spill. I'm trying to be a supportive friend for you. Something I've never even attempted before."

"Is it because I'm rich and have a magic castle?" I joke. "Because, I'm sorry, but I'm not going to be your sugar mommy."

She shoves my shoulder with hers. "Piss off, you bitch," she huffs. "But you are more likeable as a rich princess, I'll admit that. Now tell me, what the fuck happened?"

I tug at the band of blood red fabric around my chest, which is too tight, and hope I don't trip on the matching long skirt that falls from my hips to my feet. The Fire Court fashion is very revealing, so I've learnt, but it's nice to be able to breathe in my clothes. Hope looks boiling hot in her short-sleeved black top and tight leggings. I tell her everything as we walk throughout the castle, a castle she clearly knows better than I do.

Eventually she leads me out to a balcony that

overlooks the many lava pits, the looming massive volcano in the distance. I'm not sure where the people of the court exactly live—everything is just full of lava. Hope has been silent for at least ten minutes, a personal record for her, and I clear my throat as I breathe in the smoke scent. "Where is the city?"

"The city is behind here on the other side of the castle. There are a few villages, but most live in the city. It is spread out within the mountains," she explains. "They live next to the lava, and they make food on the fires. They respect the volcano, which fuels their power."

"I hope Arden wants to show me it in the future," I whisper, a bitter sting in my chest.

"Lysander fucked up, and you fucked up by not telling Arden everything before you were forced to," she states, stepping to my side. "But I've annoyingly learnt you love them, really love them, and you should fight for that. You have been through so much together."

"It's my fault." I pick at my nails. "And how could Arden want me after this?"

"Insecurity is overthinking gone wrong. Ask him. I'm certain he will want you." She wipes a hand across her forehead. "I really prefer the Water Court."

I know I shouldn't speak about Lysander with her, but it slips out. "And Lysander's cut himself off from me, from our bond. I can barely feel him, but I know he's in pain. I should go to him too."

Her shoulders tense for a second. "Let him stew about what he has done. It's strange without Grayson and Emrys to make a wall between them, like they always have. They always had rivalry growing up, and I always thought they were less friends and more just acquaintances, but they had each other's back. I never thought Lysander would want to kill him. Arden called Ly a brother. It surprises me that he did this. Even for him, this is bad."

I nod. "It surprised me too when I got to know them. I don't think he actually wanted me to kill him. Deep down, I think he would have stopped me if I had gone through with it. He would have stopped himself, too. As bitter as he makes himself out to be, he's not. I mean, I can literally feel his emotions, feel his soul. I know it's not all made with cruelty."

She sadly smiles at me. "I know that too, but he doesn't, and that's the problem. He wants himself to be the villain so badly that he won't possibly let anyone see the light, see the goodness that he got from his mum, not just the wickedness from his father."

"I'm sorry. You're the last person I should be talking about Lysander with," I mutter.

Hope touches my arm. "It's fine, really. I'm growing as a person, or trying to. I'm going to sleep and then train in the morning if you want to join me. We can get even over training as I kick your ass."

I laugh. "I was trained by the god of nightmares about how to fight. You might not want to train with me now. It won't be just muscle memory kicking in."

"Sounds like I want lessons from you then," she says with a wink, walking to the door. "As for Arden, his father's laboratories are down those stairs. Whenever he's angry, he usually goes there to think. No one else goes down there. It's pretty terrifying."

I look at the stairs. She is right; he is down there. "Thank you, Hope."

"It's annoying that I like you," she replies, walking away.

I laugh again. "I find it annoying too!" Her laugh echoes to me as she heads down the pathways, and I'm left alone with the bright orange lava, spitting fire, and endless night skies. I'm starting to realise that Hope is becoming my friend and I care about her. It's really strange considering I hated her when we met. If Hope and I can become friends, then anything is possible, and I have to face Arden.

I walk down the steps. I feel Arden closer with every step, knowing he must sense that I'm here too. At the bottom of the steps are two glass doors, thick glass that's heavy to open, but I pull on one and step inside. It's a laboratory, full of desks and smothered with strange potions on lined shelves, twisted tubes, and bubbling fires. There's a strange smell of chemicals in the air, and he is here. Arden. He has his back to me, every single one of his muscles tense under a dark red shirt as he works at the desk. His sleeves are rolled up, his black hair tied at the base of his neck, and he goes still. "Can I come in?"

"Considering you've already stepped through the door, my answer is kind of a moot point." I smile at his joke, but he doesn't look back at me. "I know you've been through a lot of shit recently, so it's really best you just don't come any closer while I'm mad. I don't want to say anything to upset you, and I need to calm my thoughts down. My dragon…

it's not happy. You're our mate, princess, and you lied to me."

His words cut deep. "I don't want that." I walk closer. "I want us, a genuine relationship, the reality of it all. We can't hide from each other when it gets messy." He pauses what he was doing, placing his hands on the desk and bowing his head.

Running my hand over his back, I slide in between the desk and him, my ass touching the cold metal desk. My heart is racing as I look up at my mate, my fire dragon king. He looks down at me with his fire red eyes, just so utterly beautiful and so hurt. "Talk to me. Please."

He watches me as I place my hands on his chest, messing with his buttons, breathing in his firewood scent. "You chose him over me. You chose to protect his secret, his mistake, over telling me the truth."

I blink. "I didn't choose him over you, Arden. At first, when he blackmailed me, I said yes because I didn't know you as anything but the kidnapping dragon who burnt a man in front of me. Can you remember that I didn't know you, not at all, and for me, it was easy to pick my grandmother over a stranger? I didn't do what he asked. I chose you over my family. I picked you, my love for you, over what my destined mate wanted me to do. The thought of hurting you is sickening to me. I hate that I hurt you by trying to protect you. I should have told you with the riders, when I had many chances, and it was wrong of me not to have done. I thought I was protecting you, because I knew the truth would hurt."

"Like I did to you, sending you to Earth?" he whispers.

"We have both fucked this up," I mutter, leaning up to him. He doesn't need any more encouragement before he kisses me deeply, passionately. Any space between us is gone, washed away. We might both be broken, but we can fix each other's cracks.

I moan into his mouth, pulling at his belt, and he places his hands over mine. "Are you sure, after—"

Pushing away from the desk, I slide to my knees. "I know what I want and what I want to forget." Arden is still as I finish undoing his belt on my knees. He digs his hands into the desk as I pull down his trousers, boxers too, until his cock is in front of me. The desk groans with how hard he grabs it when I wrap my hand around the base of his cock and suck the tip into my mouth. I know we should talk. We shouldn't be doing this to solve our problems, but I need him close. After everything, I need him to show me that I can have him.

"Princess, fuckkk," his moan echoes around the room. I don't make him wait before I sink my mouth down his cock, as far as I can go, but damn, he is long, and he hits the back of my throat far too quickly. I use my hand to stroke up and down the base of him as I work the top of his cock with my mouth, feeling him tense with every stroke, noticing his every move. I barely get to suck on him for a minute before he is pulling back, lifting me up, and turning me over the desk. He pushes up my long skirt, rips off my underwear, and pulls my legs apart. Leaning over me, he strokes his hand up to my core. "You're soaking my fingers, Ellelin."

"Then do something about it," I suggest, looking at him over my shoulder. His eyes flash with the challenge, and he lines his cock up. In one thrust, he is inside me, and he feels so perfect. I moan as he ruthlessly fucks me on his desk, every thrust moving the entire desk across the floor until it hits the wall and it has nowhere else to go. Neither of us notices the desk much, and I can only focus on the feel of him inside of me, the need to come so badly that it almost hurts. "Arden, please. I need—"

"I know what you need. You're mine," he

growls, biting down on my shoulder, his hand sliding between the desk and my core. He rubs my clit fast, and I'm crashing into an orgasm within moments.

"Arden!" I cry out his name as I come around his cock, tightening around him, and he thrusts two more times before going still, coming hard inside me. He lifts me, turning me on the desk and holding me against his chest as we both calm down.

I draw circles on his chest, noticing the grooves in the metal of the desk. "I think we broke the desk."

Arden chuckles and holds me tightly. "It's just become my favourite desk. Those are marks of honour to me."

I shake my head, grinning up at him as he lets me down. "Are we okay?"

After I finish pulling down my skirt and tidying my top, he pulls me into his arms. "I love you, Ellclin. No more secrets. We are okay."

I clear my throat. "Lysander—"

"I don't want to talk about Lysander with you. Not yet," he interrupts, and his tone makes me stop. We have pushed enough today.

"How about you show me your rooms here?

What's your favourite place of yours in the court?" I change the subject. "The Fire Court is so beautiful."

"Like you are. This is my favourite place, second to being inside you," he states, waving his hand around, making me chuckle. "It was my father's place, but it's now mine. I feel closer to my parents when I work in here. The door is spelled to scare unwanted visitors."

I look around. It didn't scare me away, so he let me in. Even upset with me, he wanted me to find him. God, I love him. Science was never a strong subject for me at school, or even one I understood well. "What do you make in here?"

"Cures, potions, changing elements from one thing to another." I can feel the excitement in his every word. He shows me a load of rocks, some of them absolutely dazzlingly beautiful. "We mix magic and elements together here to fix things too, like this, for example." He shows me a small purple potion. "I invented this. About twenty years ago, there was an outbreak of a deadly virus. I'm not sure what you call them on Earth. It spread fast and killed dragons, young and old. No one could figure out what it was. My father worked on it for years. Two years ago, there was another outbreak, and I figured out this cure. It took me a while, a lot of experimenting, but no one died. I kept the ones that had caught it alive and stopped the spread across my kingdom. I regularly trade cures with the other courts and mix their knowledge with mine so we can keep disease at bay."

My smile is wide. "That's amazing and—"

I pause mid-sentence, hearing Terrin shout a warning in mind: "Danger is coming for you." Terrin. I miss him and wish I could simply just take myself to the Spirit court to be near him, but I can't do that. Not yet. I know going back to the Spirit Court will be different, meaningful to my people there, and I want to be able to have a way to permanently fix what my father did. It doesn't make it any easier not to be with Terrin, doesn't push the ache away. He is my mate, and our bond is strong even with the distance. Even with the Spirit Court magic hanging between it. Speaking to him in my mind is like shouting at a great distance, underwater, and even then it's hard to hear.

"Terrin just said—"

"I heard him in your mind," Arden interrupts, taking my hand and leading me towards the door. "You can hear in my mind, too. Just reach." I hear a dragon roar, echoing loud above the castle, calling for us. "I'm used to dragon roars, but that sounds nothing like anyone in my court."

"Let's go outside and face this," I suggest. There is no point ignoring whoever it is. Terrin is annoyed at whoever it is, but we are too far apart to communicate well. Arden goes out and jumps off the balcony, shifting into his massive black, red-tipped, scaled dragon before swinging around and floating near the steps. After climbing the banister, I get onto his back, and he shoots off into the sky.

Suddenly a dragon slams straight into us, going straight for Arden's throat, and I can't see anything but darkness. Before it can dig its teeth in, I throw my shadows at the dragon's face and it roars, falling off and into the sky. Arden spins so fast I barely manage to hold on before he straightens in the air. The black-scaled dragon, slim and fast, reappears, flying directly in front of us. I know this dragon. It's the commander's dragon. My blood runs cold as I look across to see Tsar Aodhan on her back. For a moment…I thought the commander would be sitting there.

He's dead.

He's dead.

Aodhan shouts, his voice reaching me through

the wind. "You took my army of dragons! You killed my brother. You're a stealing fucking witch!"

Arden roars, flames spitting between us in a clear threat. I shout right back. "He deserved to die for what he tried to do to me. Do you know what he did?"

"I heard rumours. It's not like him, he didn't do it. You're a liar, sent to my army to kill and steal," he snarls. The sky is quickly filling with Fire Court dragons surrounding him. "You even spelled my dragon into breaking our bond and leaving with the army. The only loyal dragon left is my brother's." She snarls at me to make a point.

"I do not lie. And they're my army now!" I shout back. It's quiet enough that he hears every word. "They're my people, my court, and they always have been. Whether they ride or not, they do not belong to you."

His look will haunt me, the pure anger and promise of revenge. "I don't know what's going on in your courts, but I'm coming for you. One day, one time, when you don't expect it, I will ruin your life."

Arden's voice fills my head. "I can kill them. They won't touch you."

"No, let him go. He has a wife and a child. Time

will make him forget and move past this," I answer, watching Scathitine fly away with my new enemy.

Arden grumbles, flying in the other direction, back to the castle. "If he comes back to the courts, he's dead. No second chances."

Something about the look in that dragon's eyes tells me I will see them again and I will regret letting them go. She is Terrin's sister, and I can't help the swell of disappointment I feel knowing she didn't choose to fight for Terrin and me. She chose the tsar and his lies. Terrin will have to speak to his sister, make her see sense. I will ask him about it when I see him next.

We land back on the balcony, Arden shifting back. There is a guard waiting for us, and he bows to Arden. "We have news. The Earth Court is under attack from the gods."

Grayson.

CHAPTER 10

LIVIA

I thought being back on Earth, being back in my parents' home, would make me feel settled. I thought it would make the horrors of the past wash away so I could make fresh memories, but it didn't work. If anything, I'm itching, *itching* to do something, to claw that bond to my dragon out of my chest that keeps begging me with every breath to go back to another world. I think I made a mistake, but how can I go back to that world now? A world where it is clear that death is only the parting gift. I rest my head back on one of the twin rocking chairs on the wrap-around porch in the back garden and look to the sun for a clue of what I should do.

My mum's yorkie dog sits up and barks right

before running around in circles, chasing something invisible. Sadly, my mum's dog acting demented is the most interesting thing to happen in weeks.

"You look bored, mortal."

I jump out of my skin, looking over to see a man sitting in the other rocking chair on the porch. He's a man…but more. I'm utterly terrified as I meet his dark, dark eyes that flash between silver and black. They stay silver the longer I look at him. He's gorgeous, absolutely stunning, but terrifying in equal amounts. His eyes are black pits of nothing, and I can't look away as I'm trapped completely in fear. He looks away from me first, and it's only then that I seem to be able to breathe. I lean back in my seat, clutching the armrests. "My name is Phobos, and if I wanted to hurt you, you would be screaming by now. Relax."

"Phobos," I breathe, the name familiar. "The god of nightmares?"

"Among other horrors," he taunts.

"Ellelin talked about you. You're her uncle, right?" I question, wondering what the heck he is doing on my mother's porch.

"And you're her friend," he replies. "I need someone to go back to Ayiolyn with something.

Something precious. Can you be of assistance, mortal?"

His voice is normal, but it still sends chills down my spine. I want to run from him, right into the forest at the back of the garden, and pray another god saves me. "I'm not sure."

He looks annoyed. "I can convince you." Dark shadows fill the bottom of the porch, and I snap my feet up on the chair.

"Phobos!" a woman shouts, sounding pissed. She walks through my gate and storms up to the god of nightmares, facing him down like he isn't scary. "Did you leave me outside the front so you could terrify her before I came in?"

This girl is clearly mortal, about my age, and loves the colour black. She is wearing fishnet tights, a small black skirt, and a leather blouse. Her black hair is tied up in a ponytail, and she looks over at me, sighing and then rolling her eyes at Phobos before facing me again. "Hello, I'm Phobos's mate, Nevaeh. I'm very mortal and not scary like him." She offers me her hand. I shake her hand, unable to do much else. "I really hope he didn't terrify you too much. He gets too much joy in that shit."

I nervously smile at her. "You're easier to talk to, that's for certain."

Nevaeh leans on the rocking chair, and Phobos snakes his hand possessively around her waist. "What Phobos is trying to say is that Ellelin needs this sword in the future, and it is dangerous to send it with a stranger. You're friends, clearly, and we need your help. Phobos cannot go into that world; otherwise, he would go himself. So, this is his very creepy way of asking for help."

"I wasn't going to play nice with a coward who abandoned her friends and went home," Phobos drawls, and I see red.

"I'm not a coward. I've been to hell and back in that world!" Oh my god, I'm shouting at a literal fucking god.

"Unless you've met Hades, you have not been to hell and back," he quips. "That guy has gone on one male mission to being the most boring shit alive."

My mouth parts. "Hades and hell are real?"

"Of course," Phobos answers in a way that makes me think he believes I'm dumb. I don't know what to say for a long time. Phobos cuts the silence by making a sword appear out of darkness. It's covered up with a leather wrap from hilt to tip, and yet something is so wrong about the blade. "If you take this, you must not look at the uncovered sword.

It's only for one of my bloodline to wield. Do you understand?"

"I haven't said I'm going back," I retort.

"You have." He waves his hand and, right before my dog, a portal appears. On the other side, I can see the Spirit Court castle. In the skies, the fields and everywhere are dragons. My heart leaps as my bond flares to life, telling me my dragon is close, and I stand.

Tears fill my eyes. "The dragons are there."

"They came to fight for their princess. The question is, are you going to fight?" Phobos asks, his question haunting me for an answer. "I've been looking into this world. They have the castle back, and it is safe for you. The dragons burned any of the remaining traitors, and the magic castle flung the rest out the windows for the dragons to eat as snacks. It was amusing to see."

"It was disgusting," Nevaeh exclaims, shaking her head.

He shrugs his shoulder, waiting for me. "Are you going back, or shall we leave?"

My heart pounds as I know my choice. Ellelin needs me and I'm not hiding here on Earth anymore. It was a mistake to ever do that in the first place. Ellelin didn't hide, she stood up tall and faced everything. I push down my fear of that world, of death itself, and lift my head. "I need to gather some things to take."

Sarcasm laces Phobos's words. "Please take your time. We have all day."

Nevaeh hits his chest, and he pulls her onto his lap with a growl. "He means to say you can take your time, as you might not be back for a while."

"I think you're a very good translator for him." I grin at her, and the dark look that Phobos gives her sends chills through my blood. Thankfully, his mate distracts him from glaring at me as I pick up my dog and head inside. After feeding the dog, I grab the bag that I left packed, full of weapons, in my room. I stuff it with some food, a bottle of water, and my daggers from the camp, and then change back into my leather clothes for fighting. I had it all ready, just in case. I write a quick note for my mum and dad, explaining that I've gone back, that I need to go back, but I know they didn't want me here anyway. I think, before my return, they had fully accepted that I was gone, that I was meant to go to that world to find my destiny.

I don't belong here anymore.

When I'm done, I go back out into the garden and hold my hand out for the sword. Thankfully, it's got a handle, and I quickly slip it over my shoulder, so it rides on my back. It's a heavy sword, but the weight of it lies heavily in the magic I feel radiating down my spine. I want to drop it somewhere immediately. "Tell my niece to come and see me soon. Tell her the sword is from her father, entrusted to me. I could not give it to her until she was ready, and now she is."

I nod once. "I will make sure she gets this and the message."

Phobos and Nevaeh disappear, leaving me alone in the garden with a magic sword and a portal to another world. I step through the portal back into Ayiolyn without another thought, to the world that I missed. As odd as it sounds to me, I completely, utterly miss this world. The portal disappears behind me as I stand in front of the castle, looking up at the tall towers stretching into thick clouds.

Terrin lands right in front of me, his black wings spread far. I look up at the massive dragon stretching his wings out in front of me. My silver dragon lands by my side, watching me with her eyes full of sadness. I didn't expect that; I thought she hated me. "I didn't want to leave you."

"You returned, my rider." My dragon shoots off,

and anger floats down our bond. We are going to have to work on that.

Terrin brushes his head against mine, and for a moment, I can hear him in my head like my own dragon. "Why are you back?"

I lift my head. Sometimes it's the simplest answer, the one spoken right from the heart, that matters. "For the princess. To fight for my friend."

CHAPTER 11

*I*t's been two days since the fire test. Two long, excruciating days as we try to work out where exactly to go in the Earth Court. Grayson once told me that his people would be good at hiding and that no one came into the Earth Court without a guide. He wasn't joking. Arden and his people are lost when it comes to the maps of the Earth Court, or lack of them. The Earth Court is a mysterious place, and it's not until Aphrodite leaves a portal that we can even turn up. How did they manage to find where the court is and take it over so easily? Arden has been to it, but only through portals. He's pacing at my side, both of us thinking the same things. "It's a trap. She must be getting pissed that you've won two tests now."

I touch his shoulder, and he pauses, looking down at me. "It's Gray. I'm going."

"I know." He blows out a breath, touching my cheek. "The Earth Court could arguably be one of the most dangerous courts. They keep their secrets in the secret cities, buried deep within the ground. It's like a maze, Gray once told me, and only the king can know the way around it. A mind map is inherited by each king, so the court is kept safe. That portal could drop us anywhere, and we would be lost in millions of miles of mazes."

"Sounds brilliant." I drop my shoulders. "It's time to get Grayson back. We can't just ignore the portal, no matter the danger. I'm going for my Gray. He needs me." Arden doesn't argue, leading me to the throne room. People bow as we walk past them, and some gawk at me, making me want to fiddle with the tight black armoured clothes I'm wearing. "Lysander should be here, maybe—"

"I'm here."

Arden goes deadly still as we both look behind us, watching as Lysander walks down the Fire Court like he isn't the enemy, like he hasn't done anything wrong. Oh, Lysander. His head is held high, like nothing's happened, and he only stops when he is right in front of me. Lysander meets Arden's fiery gaze, and both of them growl. "I would not leave you alone to face this."

"Oh, now you're honourable," Arden sarcastically snaps with enough fire that I almost flinch away from them both.

"Enough." I slip in the middle of them. They both leave zero space between my body, like they can claim parts of me with only their touch, and magic seems to lace the air I breathe with its own threat. They are huge, massive dragon shifters, and I feel like a tiny powerless human in the middle of them.

I'm not powerless. My shadows swirl around my feet, climbing up my legs and pushing them both a few steps back. "I mean it, enough! We have a lot to face today, and this is for Grayson, who you both care about. Right?" I turn to look at them both once, my shadows still dancing around me. "He's not betrayed you, but he needs us. So does Emrys. We are going to put all of our problems behind us and go into another extremely deadly test as allies. I can't fight the fucking gods and you two as well. I will break. I am holding on with everything I have to fix your mistakes by leaving me behind in the first place. So, unless you want that outcome, stop this."

Both of them stay quiet. Lysander nods, looking at Arden. I follow his gaze, and a tic in Arden's jaw pulses once, but he lowers his crossed arms. "For you, Ellelin, I would do anything. Even work with him today."

"Thank you," I whisper, letting my shadows go. We all head towards the throne room in the most awkward silence.

Lysander clears his throat, breaking the uncomfortable moment. "This might be more of a fight than we realise. Aphrodite might not let us enter the test with you, Elle. In the last test, she was welcoming to us both because it played a part in what she wanted." Arden looks at him in disdain, but he says nothing, moving his gaze away. He tugs the throne room doors open, and I walk in, pondering Lysander's warning.

"I'm not going to leave her side," Arden states once we are all in the throne room, shutting the door behind us.

"Neither am I," Lysander claims. "Her safety is everything to me."

Arden shakes his head in disbelief. "Where were you when she was nearly attacked two days ago by a revengeful dragon and rider? If you cared, you would have been there like I was."

"What do you mean, attacked?" Lysander turns to me, searching my face like the answer is written there. "Why didn't you call for me? One word in my mind and I would have come for you. It only takes one word from you."

This is all giving me a headache, and the hard part of the day hasn't even begun. "I'm fine, let's just… We'll talk about it later." I look at the portal swirling right in front of the throne that's been waiting for us for the last hour. "Come on, we should go. I hate every second she has Grayson and Emrys under her spell."

Arden and Lysander take my hands as we step through, and immediately I know we're underground, far underground. The air is filled with a damp, musty earth scent, but mostly all I can smell and see are blue flowers. Shiny azure flowers line every wall, thousands of them bursting out of green vines. They cover every single wall, ceiling, and pillar in the massive room. There's no natural light down here, but there are big beams of light coming out of circles on the ground, in rows leading to the back of the room.

It's a massive cavern with dirt walls, and even when little grows here this far underground, it feels like a greenhouse with the smell and humidity. The earth throne itself is one gigantic piece of slate with carved-in seats, and giant, tall, spiralling wood sticks line the back of it. They make the shape of a harp, with gold strings coursing through the wood, glowing softly.

The ground is covered in blood, and the smell of death is lingering over the beauty. The portal snaps shut behind us, leaving us in the empty silence of the throne room. Aphrodite and Ares are where they always are, like they rule the court, sitting on the green cushioned seats of the throne. The throne room is empty this time. Not a single person, not even a ghost, seems to lie in the many seats at the sides. The ground itself is a meadow of thick grass and more blue flowers that have made a pathway straight down the middle. The flowers themselves seem to glow red with the blood splattered on them, but even then, they're absolutely beautiful.

I never would have guessed that Grayson's throne room is the most beautiful throne room in Ayiolyn. I look at Grayson, the king of the Earth Court, on his knees, and my heart hurts. Grayson has always needed to be in control of everything, down to even how he is touched, and the gods are using him like a puppet.

Ares watches with so much hate it burns

between us like a living thing. "Is your mother dead yet?"

"Wouldn't you like to know?" I taunt as we walk closer, stopping near Gray.

His sinister smile spreads. "She's alive, I can tell from your eyes. Such frustration. She won't wake. It's not possible. I linked her to me."

"What does that mean?" I demand, making the room dip into darkness at the edges without me even trying to.

Ares looks at the shadows near him, the way they are hissing like snakes ready to snap at his neck. "Keep begging me and maybe I might grant you an answer. I'm glad you stole her from me. She was annoying to drag around. Dead weight usually is."

He laughs as I head forward, only getting a few steps before Arden stops me, tugging me back with our joined hands. "Whatever you've done, I'll break it. You're a sick bastard, you know that?"

"Family games, such fun." He continues to laugh, and Aphrodite simply watches us both like we are a show of *EastEnders* or something. "How is my backstabbing daughter?"

"Better without her parents, I'd wager," I snarl.

"You talk about a family like you know the meaning of it. You don't."

Ares goes silent, moving to stand, but Aphrodite beats him. She rises up off her seat, her red dress moving with her. A princess gown this time. "Welcome, Ellelin. Do you like the Earth Court?"

"Where's this next test?" I snap. I'm not doing small talk with her.

"Two down, two to go. I like the number three. It's my favourite," she begins. "Three is meant to be a number that signifies unity. You three are definitely not unified after our last attempt. You can practically taste the anger rippling off your bones, the thick tension I could feed off."

No one replies to her. She wants us to fight and argue. It makes it easier for her to win. "How interesting you all are! Love really does conquer all, even betrayal. Will it conquer death?"

"Get on with it, bitch," Lysander growls.

Aphrodite narrows her eyes. "So rude. The Fire Court and Water Court kings are not welcome in this test. It would be cheating to allow you in."

"No! We do not leave her side!" Lysander shouts.

Arden looks at me, seeing the worry in my eyes.

I can't do this without them, I need them. "We are not leaving—"

"That was not part of my agreement." Aphrodite clicks her fingers, and a portal opens underneath both Arden's and Lysander's feet. Their hands are ripped out of mine as they disappear in the portals, and I'm left touching the dirt ground within seconds. They are literally just gone. "Get up."

I can do this. I have to do this. I reach for their familiar presence in my mind, and even thousands of miles away, I can feel my mates. I'm never really alone. I haven't been, and they are with me wherever I go. Steeling my back, knowing they're going to be mighty fucking pissed, I stand up and face my enemy. The goddess who needs to be stopped.

She smiles, her painted red lips bright. "I put them back in their own courts. Wouldn't want them to kill each other without your presence there to stop it." She looks at Grayson. "Earth king, you're needed." She clicks her fingers again, and he stands, walking to me. "He loves you, that one, more than the others. You're the beginning and end of his world. I've been in his mind, felt his love, and it is sad he might die in this test. Grayson will lead you to the entrance to the test. It's here within the Earth Court. It turns out this place is dangerous enough on its own without my help. But I spent the last two days devising something truly spectacular here, worthy of the gods. You might even need to be a god yourself to win it."

Ares sneers at me. "But you're not, mortal. Mortals die, and gods? We live forever."

Grayson walks to my side, my heart pounding. He doesn't reach out for me; he doesn't move much more, and he still has that red haze on his eyes from her magic. His hand moves to the small of my back, and he pushes me forward. I look over my shoulder at Aphrodite as she sits back on the throne, a big smile on her face. "Good luck, princess."

My heart feels lodged in my throat as Grayson leads me out of the throne room, through massive, decorated wooden doors and into empty corridors with little light pooling at the edges through cracks in the earth. I feel Arden and Lysander reaching for me, Terrin too, but they are so far away that it's nothing more than a faint echo. I can't tell them I'm fine; I can't shout back. I'm lost in my own thoughts, and soon I realise the corridor seems to have changed just as we have walked down it. It doesn't look the same.

Maze.

The Earth Court is a maze. I'm instantly lost.

Every wall is dark mud and looks the same, and there are no markers or signs. No way to know one corridor from the next. Within minutes, it feels like I'm lost and alone, even with the Earth Court king at my side. Grayson keeps walking, robotically, before we come to a pair of metal gates. Two people are dead outside the gates, Earth Court guards by the look of their uniforms. I try not to stare at them too long, knowing I need to focus. I hate how dead bodies aren't all that shocking to me anymore. Grayson opens the gates, and I instantly feel the magic of this place, dark, engulfing magic wrapping around me. It reminds me of Grayson, earthy and strong.

As Grayson steps in behind me, the gates slam shut behind him, sealing us in before they disappear into the dirt, like there weren't gates there at all. I look up at Gray, the red haze fading from his brilliant silver eyes. He looks down at me, his smile widening as he reaches for me, pulling me close to him in a tight hug. I'm not used to being hugged by Grayson. Not like this. Not with my entire body pressed against his hard one. He hugs me so tightly. "You're alive. You're alive."

He keeps repeating it as I breathe in his scent and hug him back. It's hard to be mad at him about the leaving me on Earth thing when he is shaking and clinging to me. The king who doesn't like to be touched is not letting me go. "I missed you too, Gray."

"You came back," he breathes down my neck, softly kissing my skin.

I shiver, his kiss like a branding that shoots pleasure through my body. "Let's not discuss that right now. Do you know where we are? It's a test."

"Doesn't matter," he mumbles into my neck. "I know—" He lifts his head, and he looks around. If I ever thought I'd seen Grayson scared before, I hadn't. Not like he is when he looks back at me, pushing off me. "NO! Not here, anywhere but here." He slams his fist into the wall. "NO! NO! NO!"

He falls down to his knees, shouting no over and over. My heart cracks at the fear in his voice. Where the fuck are we? "Grayson!" I grab his shaking, sweaty hands. Blood coats his knuckles, but I don't care. "Grayson, look at me. You're okay. It's me, Ellelin. Your Ellelin. Come back to me from wherever you are." He breathes in deep, finally lifting his head. His eyes are filled with tears, but none dare drop between us. "Okay, what is this place?"

"It's called the Labirinto," he whispers, like

words are a weapon here, and he looks around. "It's a deadly maze, built before even the courts were created. My mother used to bring me here, a lot, and she loved it here. It used to lure her in, my father said, but he didn't know about it until it was too late. They say a mighty dragon god died in this place, and his spirit made the maze as a way for him to live and torment. This place, it…makes your worst fears come true, makes you see things that are not there while promising you your dreams. My mother went mad in this place. I was with her, trapped with her for months. While she slowly went mad, my father couldn't get me out. No one in the court could get me out. So, she just hurt me over and over again, not even aware of who I was in the end. She just thought I was an enemy sent to hurt her. For so many months, it was just me and her bumping into each other again and again. I wouldn't hurt her back, and sometimes I went to her, knowing she would hurt me but just needing to speak to someone. Anyone. I was only five; I needed my mum."

Sickness rises in my throat as my heart shatters for him. I knew he had scars on his body, that he went through something terrible, but I didn't know it was this. This is worse than I ever could have imagined. "That's why you didn't want to be touched anymore. How long were you in here?"

"A year." The two words crumble between us as horror lances my heart. "I was trapped in here for a year. The scars…she made weapons and used to cut me every time to make the darkness get out of my blood, as she put it. She found me, thought she could drain evil from me. I don't know how to explain to you what it's like to have your mother not even recognise you and hurt you over and over again. I never wanted to come back to this place. I locked it up and guarded it so that no one would ever get in and out."

I stroke his palm. "How did you get out in the end? How did you and your mother get out in the end?"

"To this day, I do not know how I got out. It just finally let me out a year later. Maybe this place was bored with me. I'd all but given up by then and was thinking of ending things," he admits, and he looks up. "I'm glad I didn't. I wouldn't have met you, the greatest reason for living I've ever known."

"Gray," I whisper, searching his eyes and moving closer to him. "And your mother?"

He looks beyond me, at the walls of ivy that

make the maze. "She wandered out too, but she was never the same."

"Grayson…I'm sorry. I'm so, so sorry. How did your father deal with it all?" I whisper. As a child, no one spoke about the Earth Court, around me at least. I never met Grayson or his parents as a child.

"It broke what was left of my father's soul when we came home. My mother never came home mentally. It was like this place stole her soul. And when my father couldn't even hug his son, and his son wouldn't let anyone touch him? He tried his best to heal me, to be a righteous king, but he couldn't. He wasn't exactly the greatest person at being kind and loving. But he tried with me. I think a part of him left when we went missing, and that part never came home either." He sighs softly, pulling me onto his lap. I wrap my arms tightly around him, leaning on his chest, listening to his racing heart. "You can always hug me. It doesn't… I'm not scared of you. I will never be scared of you. We need to get out of this place, Ellelin."

"Do you remember how you did it all those years ago at all?" I ask once again. Anything would be useful at this point.

"No, there was nothing memorable to it. I just woke up one morning, and the door was there. It didn't make any sense. The mystery of it almost drove my father insane. He sent so many people in here to get my mother out, to get me out. Hundreds. They were never seen again. At the beginning, it was volunteers happy to try to save the prince and queen. After a few hundred, the volunteers waned, and no one wanted to come in here. Can you blame them?" I shake my head. "So my father just started sending people in. You can say, when he died, there wasn't much cheer for his life, for their ruler. Many didn't want me either, 'the broken maze king,' they named me."

"Love cripples people sometimes," I whisper.

He leans in, brushing his lips across mine. I gasp at the contact, at the amazing feeling from just a brush of his lips. A slow dance that takes my breath away. "I understand him now. I never did, not until you were taken from me at the end of the Dragon Crown Race. To not know what happened to the woman you love…madness becomes a friend. I think he loved my mother. Dearly loved her. From what I remember, she was a good person, but…it's all bled into misery. I have a little sister who is her image. I've tried to bring her up, and when we are out of here, I'd like you to meet her. She is safe. I hid her with guards before the Dragon Crown Race, just in case it went wrong."

Madness, it's what I felt on Earth at the thought of never seeing them again. "I love you, Grayson. I wanted you to know that I loved you from the first training session, from the first time you were vulnerable with me. I didn't know what it was I felt for you, but it's just grown, and now you are part of me. You always will be. I don't see you as broken, Gray, I see you as my perfect king."

He kisses me again. This time it's different. A desperate passion, his hands digging into my hair. He breaks the kiss, looking deep into my eyes. "I love you with every crumbled inch of my scarred heart."

The ground shakes violently, and Grayson pulls me to my feet with him. Aphrodite's voice echoes loudly. "Find the monster and destroy it to be free!"

We run just as the ground cracks under our feet. Grayson reaches a hand out to stop the ground splitting under us, but nothing happens. "She has taken my powers, or this place has!" I try to call on my shadows, but they don't move. We both leave the idea of using magic to help us, and run through the maze, around the ivy-walled corner, as the ground cracking follows us.

My heart pounds, thinking of Grayson in here, being chased by his own mother. He and Lysander have a lot in common with their fucked-up parents and childhood. I was lucky my parents never did any of that. I never once felt scared when I was in their presence, and I can't imagine what it'd be like to feel scared like that.

We're just going around a corner when Grayson goes still. I hear a deep growl echoing and vibrating through the walls near us.

"What the fuck is that?" I whisper, clutching Gray's hand.

"Some of the maze is alive," he informs me. Could have mentioned that small bit of information before. Something bursts out of the ground, looking very much like a dragon, but it's made of vines, with snapping sharp green teeth, and it lunges straight at us. Grayson pushes me behind him in one swift move, and he reaches out, grabbing the mouth of this gigantic creature before it can bite him. His muscles strain against his shirt as he roars at it, and with nothing but strength, he pulls it apart with his bare hands, letting the vines shatter to the floor. Breathlessly, he looks back at me and smirks. "Their mouths are their weak place."

My heart is racing as I smile. "That was sexy."

"I aim to please you." He grins and holds my hand once more. "But we need to move right now." We run again. It feels like we run forever, for hours, when it's probably only minutes, before we come around an ivy corner to a clearing. In the centre of the clearing is a house in the middle of the maze. Grayson looks down at me in confusion for a second. "I've never seen anything like this."

It's a giant house, made of vines too. The roof is made of wicker, and it must be at least four stories high. The wooden door swings open. "It looks like something out of a horror film, and if horror films taught me anything, you don't go into the creepy house."

"We should go inside. This is a test, remember?" Grayson quietly replies.

I look behind me to see that the passageway we came through is gone, replaced with ivy walls. I rub my hand over my face. "Okay, possibly we do need to go inside there, but why do I feel like we shouldn't?"

He tightens his grip on my hand. Even with Gray at my side, I know that place is evil and we shouldn't go near it. "I feel it too. You'll be okay," he reassures me. "I'm not gonna let anything happen to you, Elle."

I blow out a breath. "I really hope you don't."

He stays close to my side as we head to the house, the feeling only getting worse. We walk up the few broken steps and through the open door into the clearly haunted house. I'm not into horror movies or anything scary, even with my uncle being the god of horror. Hell, I don't even watch horror movies on Halloween. Each step creaks and echoes as we walk inside, and we stop as the door slams shut behind us.

It's one massive room and there doesn't seem to be a downstairs or upstairs of the house, even if it looks like there is from outside. It's just one giant room. We aren't alone. On a chair in the middle of the room is an older woman. I don't need Grayson to tell me who she is. I can see from the way he goes still, everything in him seems to pause, like the world has stopped. I don't know if she's real or an illusion. Gray said this place makes you see things that are not there. Maybe it's her soul, or maybe this place lured her back here instead of the spirit castle on the night my parents died, the night we thought she died.

Suddenly, vines lash around my body, yanking me up in the air. As Grayson reaches for me, vines wrap around him too, pushing him to the side. The vines wrap around my throat, around every part of my body, and even my mouth. "Touch is a killer, son. The goddess told me who you really are, the monster I always knew. Now you have a bride, and you will make more monsters with her to fill the Earth Court unless I stop her. I promised the goddess I would stop her and teach you a lesson too."

"GRAYSON!" I shout against the vines as something begins to grow on them. Thorns. They cut into my arms and legs first, and then they stop. Until Grayson steps closer to me. I scream, my blood pouring down the vines. With every step closer to me, the thorns grow, but he can't hear me. I notice the second he realises, blood draining from his face as he goes still.

"She will die, my son, unless you free her. The thorns will pierce her heart by the time you free her," Grayson's mother, the Earth Court queen, taunts. He takes a single step towards me, and they cut deeper, and I scream around the vine in my mouth.

Grayson turns to her, fury and pity written all over his face. Sorrow too. "I'm sorry, Mother. I'm sorry you never truly got out of here and a pathetic goddess is using you. But if you don't let go of

Ellelin, I'm going to kill you, because she is my world. My touch won't hurt her, not like you hurt me." He moves away from me, and the thorns freeze. The only sound is my blood dropping on the ground, drip after drip. "Your name is Becca. Becca from Cornwall. From a small little village, a human who fought to be a dragon queen and won. You had two children, a boy and a girl, and they loved you. This shouldn't be your ending."

"Gray," I whisper, feeling weak. It shouldn't be him who does this. He goes to his mum, picking up a knife made of green rock off the ground between them. There are dozens of green knives around and, sickeningly, I realise that's what she used to cut him with as a child.

"I'm sorry," he thickly whispers, pulling his mum into a hug even as she fights him. He stabs her straight through the chest, through her heart, as he does. The vines around me fall away, and I slam onto the ground, bleeding everywhere. A roar, male and ancient, shouts over the house as Grayson begins to glow green. Softer vines wrap around me as the house cracks open, and they raise me up in the air with Grayson until we are high above the maze.

The Earth Court king has his powers back. With

a scream full of anger and fury, Grayson tears the maze apart, illuminated by flashes of green light. Through the haze of blood loss, I witness the maze being obliterated, torn to shreds by a fiery green light as if the earth is submitting to its true king. No dead god owns this land, King Grayson does, and it is finished.

When it's all silent, there is a broken metal gate left in the middle of the pit of ruins. Grayson picks me up out of the vines, holding me to his chest as everything fades to darkness, and I hear Aphrodite's scream of anger haunt me to sleep.

CHAPTER 12

I wake up to a knife at my throat, pressed against my skin, the icy blade cutting me with my every breath. The haze of everything that happened in the test comes back to my mind as I look up at the hooded figure leaning over me, wheezing with every breath. Water drops from his cloak onto my cheek, and he is heavy, pressing the blanket tightly down on my arms. I try not to panic, not to move, and reach for my mates, but they are too far away to stop him. Their panic mixes with mine until I'm not sure who is more frightened. His breath stinks as he hovers over me, cutting me more when he leans down. I don't know where I am. I don't know where my kings are. He snarls at me, and all I can see are his mud-brown eyes, thick beard, and little else. "Ares wants me to make you suffer, stupid bitch."

With a false confidence, my lips tilt up. I'm sure I can rip him away from me, but it's likely he will get a cut in before I do. "If I were you, I'd start running right about now."

His eyes muddle with confusion and a tad bit of fear, as I make every light in the room disappear. Before I can even get my shadows to protect me, which they would, vines wrap around the man's neck and arms, wrenching him back. Green light pours into the room from the doorway, just enough for me to see vines slamming the assassin into the ceiling, cutting through him in hundreds of places as he screams in absolute agony above me, blood dripping down onto the bed.

I crawl away in the darkness, watching as a shirtless Grayson steps into the room. He is stunning. Grayson's tanned chest is defined by his muscles, the ripples of his abs across his stomach, and every inch of him is covered in tiny scars. There are markings across his heart, earth symbols and small dragons, and he has a line of hair disappearing into his tight black jeans. I gulp, trying to remember I'm being attacked. Once he has looked me over from head to toe, for injuries I suspect and not the reason my horny self is staring open-mouthed at him, he seems to relax. It's like the assassin isn't screaming in agony as he smirks at me, leaning on the wall. "I left you alone for fifteen minutes after one of the female healers dressed you and healed you."

Rubbing my neck, I climb off the bed. I'm only wearing a dark green top over my bra, and I have black leggings, the outfit sticking to every inch of my body as both are a size too small. Grayson clearly hasn't seen what I'm wearing before, judging by the wide-eyed gaze and the flush of his cheeks when he looks at me. I spot a black cloak on a nearby chair and slip it on, tying up the buttons. "Ares sent him."

Grayson's vines keep cutting into him, and he screams and screams, begging for help, begging for someone to stop this. I have no sympathy for the stranger. Grayson takes my hand, tugging a shirt off the side, slipping it on. "We will find another room. I brought guards with me. They are watching outside."

He leads me outside, shutting the door behind us. There are two guards out here, in dark brown and green armour, head to toe in it, and I can't see anything more than their green eyes. There are three dead guards on the ground near them. The assassin must have killed them to get to me. Grayson touches each of their heads, leaving a green leaf marking glowing softly. A mark of respect. Grayson's voice holds no mercy when he rises. "Take him into the dungeons, torture him for information, and then kill him slowly. He tried to attack your queen, so make sure he suffers for the seconds he got alone with her." His voice lowers. "As for our fallen, their families are to be told they died bravely protecting their queen and they will be honoured by the mighty dragon gods."

"Yes, my king," the guard coldly responds. "And, my queen, rest easy, the Earth Court is yours."

Before I can even address the fact Grayson openly called me his queen, and the guards seem to think I'm the queen of their court already, three angry voices fill my mind. Arden and Lysander are in their courts, but they might as well be right in front of me. Our mental bond is insane, jumping from strong to weak. It's just as confused as I am about our relationships. "I'm fine, calm down. I'm from the shadow court and have my own powers. Even if Grayson hadn't turned up, I would have been easily able to stop him from hurting me. I just wanted to get some information from him first and know why he was trying to kill me."

"Information is not worth your pain," Arden mutters in exasperation.

"For once, the fire king is correct. Just kill the next one," Lysander all but demands. "And remind Grayson to keep you close."

"Burning them is the best way to get information. Fire makes any male scream the truth." I wince at Terrin's suggestion. He has been a dragon for far too long.

"He's not wrong," Arden starts, but I don't want to continue this discussion.

"I'm fine, all of you. Now go back to whatever you were doing and stop filling my mind with your overprotectiveness." I can sense none of them are happy, but my mind settles into a quiet.

Grayson is searching my face, even as we continue to walk. "Are they in your mind?" I nod. "They're tidying up their courts, adding further protection to the borders. Aphrodite's been sending attacks to both of them, testing the armies even now," he explains to me. "I believe even if we win these tests, she will continue to be a problem for our courts."

"Bitch," I mutter.

He kisses the side of my head, and I lean my head on his shoulder, loving and appreciating every new touch between us as we go down the pathways that are all the same. There's not a painting or statue to mark the areas. "The Earth Court is safe, and so are you. The assassin must have been left here, but I have my guards checking everywhere now, and I'm not letting you out of my sight for the night. I thought maybe you could meet my sister? The Air Court is harder to get into than others, and I believe we have tonight at least before we need to travel to Emrys's court. You could rest if you'd prefer—"

He's nervous. I take his hand, linking our fingers, and interrupt him. "I'd love to meet her. I don't think I could sleep right now anyway." I lift his hand, kissing his knuckles once. "Are you okay? We haven't had a moment to talk about everything that happened in the earth test. Did I imagine you ripping up the maze like some kind of earth god?"

"I ripped it up, let's just leave it at that." He turns us around a corner and gently pushes me into the wall, leaning into me. He kisses me softly, just a lingering brush that has me wanting so much more. "All that matters to me is that you're okay. We can do this. You have one test left. I wish I could take it for you. Part of me wants to keep you here, safe and protected at my side."

"Emrys," I breathe out.

"I know." His voice is pained. "We are one test away from our time, our future. They'll be gone. We get our world back. We can work out a future between all of us and, while we're on the subject, what happened with Arden and Lysander? Because things are tense."

"Lysander fucked up. It's complicated, but I'm glad you're here. I feel like I'm going to be suffocated if I try to keep being between them and making sure they don't hurt each other any more than they already have," I answer, and Grayson frowns. I quickly explain everything that happened, and Grayson is quiet for a while.

He tucks a strand of my hair behind my ear, sighing. "Let me guess, Lysander did it for his father."

"How did you guess that?"

"Because all of us know what his father was like and how Lysander just doesn't see it. Never did. I am good friends with his brother. I'm very glad he's alive, and his brother knows what his father was like. I believe that's a conversation Lysander needs to have with his family, to make him realise getting revenge in the name of someone like that isn't worth it."

"Maybe you can talk to him," I suggest softly. "I mean, now that I know about your childhood, perhaps you and Lysander have more in common than you know. Just don't be mad at him. I'm mad enough for all of us."

"I'm still punching the fucker for blackmailing you, but I'll try to be nice, for you." I'm not sure punching someone counts as being nice. Grayson tugs me off the wall and keeps walking. "We're sending my mother's body into the Mists in the morning, when dawn hits the highest point in the Earth Court. I would like you to be at my side for the funeral."

"Of course I will be," I quickly answer. "I'm so sorry for everything that happened to her. For her ending."

"She's been dead to me for years, an unanswered mystery that I can now put to rest. Some people said she went to the fifth court that night it exploded, but some people said she went back into the maze, that it lured her in again. Now we know. I have to admit, part of me is relieved that we finally have her body. That my sister and I can send her off. Our court can move on from that time of misery.

That deadly maze is now gone from our court, and the threat along with it. I needed it gone, and I'm glad I could destroy it. If we have any children, if I'm lucky enough that you ever decide to have one or three with me—"

"Three?" I cough on the word. Children, it's never been something I've thought about. Growing up, I was taught to fight by Phobos and to use magic by Hera, and I was raised as a fighter. To avenge my parents one day, to make it safe in Ayiolyn once more. To protect myself. Having a future, having children and a happy ending was never on my mind. I'm not sure if it's something I even want. I raise an eyebrow at him, and he laughs with me.

I like this side of Grayson. He leans into me, like it's a secret for us both, even if the world must see it. "I must be obsessed with you, because three seems like only the beginning for us. Fuck, I want everything with you. A life full of all the messy, happy, and normal things. I want your safety in my court, in our court, and I should have destroyed the maze a long time ago. I didn't realise I was even powerful enough to destroy it until I saw how you'd been hurt, and I lost it."

"I'm okay now, thanks to you," I whisper back to him. He searches my eyes before leading me around another corner, where there is a door with guards outside. The guards bow, stepping to the side. Grayson knocks once. "Come in!"

Grayson was right. His sister is the image of his mother. Long, dark brown hair that falls to her waist, several bits clipped and braided back with purple flowers. She's younger, probably getting on thirteen years old. She is still lanky in that way that I remember being just as I came into my teenage years. She stands up, her pen dropping onto the floor as she squeals in happiness. She all but throws herself at me, wrapping me in a tight hug. I'm a bit startled by her, so much so that my arms sort of stick out in the air awkwardly for a while before I hug her back. "Nice to meet you, um. Well, Grayson never even told me your name."

"Blossom," she answers with a grin that is just like her brother's. Grayson shuts the door behind us. "I feel like I know you, Ellelin. Grayson talked about you. A lot. We used to send letters back when he was in the Dragon Crown Race, and all his were about this purple-haired girl that he met. He claimed you were wildly beautiful, crazy, fierce, and brave. And when he came home, he was so different." She pauses, looking at her brother lovingly before continuing, "I thought you were too good to be true, but then you came here to go into a deadly test set up by two gods for my brother. You are a freaking badass!"

"No swearing, Bloss," Grayson orders, but it's playful.

She rolls her eyes at him and turns back to me. "You are family to me. End of. Whether you marry my brother or not. And, Gray, you'd be stupid to ever let this one out of your sight. She's far prettier than you. You're punching, so the humans say. I love your hair."

"Thank you. I used to have it all purple before. I haven't had much time to dye it, but I think I'm sticking with the black for a bit, with purple tips eventually," I explain, rambling a little. Something about her makes me a little nervous, like I need to impress her for Gray. "I'm so sorry about your mother."

"I'm glad you found her," Blossom replies, sounding so much older than she looks. "It's difficult because I don't really remember her or dad as I was a baby. I remember Gray coming back and caring for me, and stories from my caretakers of my parents." She shrugs slightly. "Tomorrow is closure for us all." I smile sadly at her, and she changes the subject. "What are you two up to tonight?"

"Someone just tried to kill me." I blow out a breath.

Grayson frowns at me. "That was not part of my plan for the night. Ares sent someone after her, but she wasn't hurt. He's not from our court. I'm not exactly sure how he got here, and he must have been left by Ares. The guards are searching the castle, the whole place now, so you must stay in your room. I'm taking Ellelin to the principal city."

"You are?" I excitedly question.

He pulls me to his side, his eyes teasing. "Do you not want to see it? We could just—"

I shove his shoulder. "No, I do want to see it. In fact, that sounds amazing. I never really got to see much of the other courts. I've just been whisked through them in a rush."

"Then I'm glad I'll be the first to show you the Earth Court." He kisses my cheek.

Blossom is smiling at us both, joy shining in her eyes. I wonder how long she has waited to see her brother happy. Grayson was never happy when we first met, and he has changed so much since we have been together. "I'll leave you two lovebirds to it." Blossom goes to the bed, and soft green vines spread out of the ground around the bed, wrapping around it and bursting with flowers. "I have to practice my magic for my tutor. Have fun and see you both soon."

"I'm leaving you in charge tomorrow when we go to the Air Court, with the nobles' guidance," Grayson tells her, leading me to the door. "Behave for them, please."

Blossom's eyes are the picture of innocence. "I'm quite happy looking after the court, brother. I'll see you in the morning."

We leave his sister's room, and Grayson leads me to a balcony. "Blossom isn't a fan of some of the nobles' sons. She dared them to race, in dragon form, around the court and when she won, she proudly made them eat enchanted sweets that turned them all gold from head to toe for a week. Their fathers were furious. I'm not sure who taught her pranks were a good idea, especially in a court full of old nobles who are serious about near enough everything, but I find it hard not to laugh when I hear what she has done."

I laugh, unable to stop myself. "I like your sister more and more. Tell me more." He does, so many stories that range from when she was just a toddler to the girl she is now, until we get to a massive balcony made out of branches of a tree. There is nothing but mountains for as far as I can see.

Grayson kisses the top of my head before he jumps off a gap in the balcony edge, shifting into his beautiful green, grey-tipped dragon. His dragon waits, watching me with his blazing silver eyes. I climb onto his back, and he swoops straight off into the sky, arching over the brilliantly tall green mountains. There is nothing but mountains here, so many of them covered in moss that shine like emeralds. They all look the same, and I guess if he didn't know better, we would be lost. I wouldn't have a clue where anything is.

Grayson dives, effortlessly flying between the mountains, his beautiful wings spread out far, and they shimmer in the moonlight. He flies over a crystal-clear lake between the mountains, with glowing gold fish swimming under the water. He runs his claws through the water, making the fish swim faster, some of them jumping out of the lake and diving back like dolphins. I laugh as cold water splashes at me before he dives high in the sky again, through the clouds, around a mountain, taking my breath away with how fast he is. Grayson's dragon moves like he is part of the mountains, of the ground and rock, and he blends so well with his surroundings that I can't imagine I'd ever see him coming.

The moonlight shines against his scales as he lands on the side of a massive mountain, leaning down to let me stand on a ledge in front of an archway before he shifts back. "I thought we were seeing the city?"

"Come, I'll show you the city. It's my favourite view from up here," he explains, taking my hand and leading me inside. It's warm inside the mountain, and I relax as fire lanterns light the way down.

"Is it one big city like it is in the Fire Court?" I question.

"No, there are five cities that make up the Earth Court. We actually have the most land in comparison to the others but not the most people. We are a court of few," he explains to me as we keep walking down the spiralling steps. The damp air grows warmer as we go down, and bright lights shine from below. "This is the capital city, Mesist," he explains to me as I blink through my adjustment to the light. "This is where it all began for the Earth Court. My great-grandfather built the first city in the mountains with just his power, clawing it out from nothing but dirt and rock. The other cities, their expansions, all connected through to this one. The very walls hold our ancestors' bones, all of them, and then the dust of the burnt bodies as time went on."

We finally get to the bottom of the steps where it's an entire crystal floor, and the crystal is completely see-through, displaying a massive city below us. The city looks like a hundred, if not more, pyramids made of dirt and rocks. There are spiralling crystals at the top of each one of the pyramids across the massive cavern floor, each a different colour and glowing like stars. Some of the pyramids are taller than others, and there are dragons wrapped round the tips, leaping on the sides, others flying through the air. "Magnificent," I gasp, but the word isn't enough to explain how amazing this city is. There are thousands of trees, pathways, and roads leading around the pyramids. There is even a river with a sand beach on the right, and I can see dots of people playing. "Is it safe in here?" I ask, looking at the crystal floor.

Grayson wraps his arms around me from behind, his mouth close to my ear. "I'll catch you if you fall, my queen." I lean into him, enjoying his touch. "No one else knows of this place. This is a sacred place for me. When I was young, after I came out of the maze, I needed somewhere safe to go to be alone. The court was always watching me for any signs of madness, always trying to fix me and talk to me, and I couldn't do it. This place appeared to me. I never thought I'd bring anyone here. I knew I'd marry, but I had no intention of actually taking a wife in every way that matters. I didn't want anyone in my life to share the secrets of my past with. But then when I met you, all I could think about was bringing you here, of sharing everything with you." He turns me around, running his hands up my back, cupping the back of my neck. "Love, it seems a fragile word for what I feel for you, Ellelin. My love for you is limitless of any words, of any one feeling that can be described. When there is nothing more than the earth left, it will be marked with the love I feel for you. We are endless, Ellelin, because you are my every dream come true."

My heart feels like it's bursting. "I love you, Gray. When we first met, I thought you were infuriating and cocky, but there was something that made me keep looking for you. The more we trained, the more I saw another side of you. You're kind, in spite of everything that happened to you, and that is so brave. You let me touch you, even when you had been taught touch could mean pain as a child. You were brave, you are brave, and I will love you forever, even if you never want me to touch you again. I'd wait, forever, Grayson."

He takes a step towards me until our bodies are flush and there isn't a gap between us. We have come such a long way since we met, when he wouldn't even let me hold his hand. Now he touches me like we are one person, linked forever, and I love it. Fear can threaten everything good in your life, but defeating fear? That lets love in. He sinks his hand into my hair. I love every moment he holds me like this, where I can breathe in his scent and claim anything I can get from him. "I've never been with a woman, but I've watched, I've learnt, and I want you."

My cheeks burn as he looks at me so intensely, waiting for my answer. "I'm yours, Gray. I've always wanted you." Gray groans, kissing me deeply, pulling me to him. I clutch his shirt as he deepens the kiss, his tongue exploring my mouth, coaxing me with every brush of his soft lips. His body is hard against mine, and all I want to do is be closer. I wonder if he can sense how wet I am from one kiss, how badly I want him. He suddenly pulls away and I frown. "Are you okay?"

"Do you trust me?" he questions, undoing the top button of his shirt, and he unclips the top of his cloak until it falls to the floor. I nod. Trusting Grayson has never been an issue for me. I used to think it was a weakness of mine, to trust the dragon kings so easily, but now I know it's more than that. I suspect Grayson and Emrys are also my destined mates, and one day the bond will kick in for us, too. I believe the only thing holding us back now is trust.

Grayson softly begins to glow green, the vibrant shade smothering the darkness in this crystal cave. Dark emerald-coloured vines break out of the walls and come to me, wrapping around my body, and I realise he is making a seat for me. The vines tug at my clothes, pulling the cloak away first and then digging into my clothes. I gasp as they rip away my leggings like they're nothing, and then my top next until I'm in nothing but my bra and panties, sitting on a chair made of vines.

The vines pull me up, almost making a bed now, and the entire time, Grayson watches me with fire burning in his eyes. He removes all of his clothes slowly, watching me as my heart races. I have to remember to trust Gray as the vines wrap around my wrists and ankles, and part my legs for his view. "One word from you, and the vines drop. You're in control as much as I am, Elle."

"Are you just going to watch?" I tease, wiggling on the vines. They tightly hold me down but not enough to hurt me, and Grayson's low chuckle sends shivers down my spine. He slowly approaches me. The green light shining off the vines lets me see all of him. His impressive cock is hard, bigger than any I've seen before, and the only part of him that isn't scarred. His scars almost seem like rays of light across his tanned skin, and they only make him more stunning. The muscles in his arms clench as he steps between my legs, running his hands up my bare thighs. I'm hyperaware we are right above a city, but I know he wouldn't let anyone see us.

He hooks his fingers in my underwear, pulling them off with one snap. Grayson looks up at me, running his hands up my flat stomach and to my bra. In one smooth pull, he snaps the bra off, and his eyes fix on my rock-hard nipples. It isn't cold in here, or I don't notice as he looks at me. I feel like I'm on fire, like my blood is lava. He runs his hands over my breasts, his scarred hands only adding to the sensations as he finds my nipples and begins to roll them both between his fingers. I moan, arching against the vines, and he growls low, sinking to his knees.

He makes the seat just the right angle and height

for him to still play with my nipples and kiss my core. I cry out in pleasure as his hot tongue swirls around my clit, once, twice, before he licks me up and down. "I wish I tasted you sooner, Elle. I don't think I'll ever get enough of you now." He speaks against my core, his voice full of amazement, and I can't take it for much longer. For someone who hasn't had sex before, he knows exactly what he is doing with my body. Grayson sucks, nibbles, and swirls his tongue around my clit at the same time as rubbing my nipples until I can't see through the pleasure. My cry echoes around the cave as my orgasm crests, slamming through my body in wave after wave until my limbs feel like jelly. Hazily, he leans over me, lining himself up and looking down at me.

"Gray," I whisper, pleading. There is hesitation in his eyes, and I know it's nothing to do with me, but to do with whatever is going on in his mind. Oh, Gray. He lets the vines go, and I wrap myself around him as he picks us up. I sit on his lap, moving myself around until I'm hovering above him. "Talk to me."

He leans his head against mine, closing his eyes. "You're a goddess to me, and I will never be sure I'm enough for you when I look like this. How could you want me when you have mates who look perfect? How can I compare?"

"Grayson." I cup his face, lifting him up to look at me. "First of all, it's not about comparing. Second…" I take his hand, placing it between my legs. "Do I feel like I don't want you?" I gasp as I push one of his fingers inside me. "I want you more than I want to breathe, Gray. I love you, and you are beautiful. I will tell you a thousand times if you need to hear it, but you're mine. You're mine and I want you." His eyes darken and he lines his cock up one more time, any hesitation gone. The tip of him brushes against my folds, feeling how soaked I am.

"I love you too and I will never deserve you, but I won't let you go," he vows against my lips, just as I sink down onto him, taking him inch by inch, watching as he groans in pleasure. It stings, how big he is, but I push through the stab of pain that is overwhelmed by the pure pleasure that courses through me as I finally take all of him. He is so still, his eyes flaring with pleasure as he pulls me to him and kisses me. "I-I can't control—"

"Don't," I whisper, and he snaps. Grayson throws me back on the bed of vines and pulls out of me, slamming right back in. I moan into his mouth as his tongue devours me, and he thrusts uncontrollably into me. My moans echo with his as I feel myself getting close again. With each thrust, he sends me closer, and he is completely lost in pleasure.

Grayson ploughs into me like a man lost, and I enjoy every second of him, every thrust, every kiss until we are completely one. His hands dig into my hips, and he bites my lip, the stab of pain sending me over the edge. I tighten around him, screaming his name in pleasure as waves of bliss run through my body. He stills inside me with a roar that shakes the cave, filling me with his cum. Breathlessly, I stare at him as he kisses me softer this time, still hard inside me, despite coming. "Again?"

I nod, a soft chuckle escaping my lips. He pulls out of me, sinking back to his knees with a devilish grin. "I'm addicted to you, Elle."

With one swipe of his tongue, I know I am, too.

CHAPTER 13

KING GRAYSON OF THE EARTH COURT

*M*y heart hurts to see my mother's silver boat float across the grey mists, into death's waiting hands. There's a smell here, one I only associate with the last moments before people die. It's sweet, like honey that's crystallised, but laced with a bitter touch of death. The Mists are spread far and wide around the mountains of the Earth Court, but they do not belong to my land or to anyone but death. To claim them would be claiming death itself. The Mists of the Dead are empty, but I sense something lurking in there, something that no one living should see.

My sister is softly informing Ellelin what this place is, how our funerals are different from how they do them on Earth. We don't bury or burn our dead very often in the courts. Most choose to be brought here to be sent away into the Mist with the mighty dragon gods. "This is the Death Mist, Elle. We send our dead in boats across so our souls can rest with the gods. The dragon gods, not the invaders to our world. Every court, mortal or dragon, sends their dead here, and it is an honour."

"It's beautiful," Ellelin whispers, her soft tone weaving around my heart like a bandage. Again, I wonder how she is so brave and how I will ever deserve her. She fixes my soul with every whispered word, with every single moment she spends in my company. Ellelin doesn't see me as a scarred monster undeserving of her, and maybe with time, I might convince my own mind not to see myself that way.

My sister stands proudly at my side, and it's good to have her here, beside me, as we say goodbye in our own way. I look down at her, the very image of my mother, and she smiles up at me for a second, her eyes glazed with tears. I want to comfort her, but I'm not sure any words I could say would help. It's hard to mourn someone you don't know, but she was our mother. She was queen of the Earth Court.

I look behind me at the hundreds of my people

in black and green, mourning with us. For a time, she was good at being a queen, but that isn't how she will be remembered. She's with my father now, her mind free of the madness, but I will never be free of her scars.

Ellelin is on my other side, and she looks up at me, her scent wrapping around me like a vice. Even at a funeral, my cock grows hard just looking at her. Now that I've been inside her, she is more addictive to me than I ever thought possible. I don't know what we've been doing with our spare time, but we definitely should be having more sex. I love her, this shadow princess of mine, and there isn't a place in any world I wouldn't be at her side.

I'm not alone in that sentiment, and fuck, I want Emrys here to help fix things. Lysander and Arden are here, both of them on opposite sides, far away from us, like even standing close to each other is an insult. They are kings of powerful courts, but more importantly, they are Ellelin's destined mates. The distance between them hurts her, and I will find a way to fix it.

I spot how Ellelin's gaze flickers between them, like a mouse caught in a trap between two giant foxes. I kiss the top of her head, breathing in her scent. "I'll catch up with you soon, my love."

Even her confused frown is cute. "Okay."

"Oh, I can show you my private rooms, and then we—" I drown out my sister's ramblings as I walk away, knowing she will be safe with the new guards I have around, who are watching them constantly for any threat. The lands have been searched for any threats, anyone showing signs of Aphrodite's or Ares's magic hold, but so far, only two have been found and killed.

Arden is heading her way, and I'm sure he will steal her from my sister soon enough. I look once more at the boat floating away, barely an outline now. The funeral is over the second she cannot be seen anymore, and there are no words to be spoken, even for a queen. We don't speak to the dead, nor do we say words to let them go in public. Those words can be spoken in private before the boat is set off, with only their spirit to hear and whisper to you. Time is nothing as I watch the boat, the Mist carrying it so perfectly. It's so quiet…until a voice whispers into my ear. At first, I don't believe it's real, I will never know if it is…but it's my mother's. "I'm sorry, my son. I always loved you, my beautiful prince. I will see you in the Mists and hug you once again. I love you, I love you…I love you." I blink and look to my side, but there is nothing but Mist there.

Needing a distraction, I walk to Lysander's side, who doesn't look impressed with anything. He never has, mind you, but something is broken now. I can't leave my brother like this, not without attempting to help. "Are you wondering if your father's in there, cursing you for not killing Arden yet?"

"You've heard," he says coldly, like I'm a stranger to him. If a good bunch of my nobles weren't staring at us, I'd punch the fucker in the arm. I keep my voice low. "You're a moron and deserve to be hung off the side of my mountains by your wings." Lysander tenses. "But you're my friend, my brother in choice, and I'm not walking away from you because you fucked up. We're going to fix it."

"This isn't fixable," he snarls at me, drawing attention. "Who says I even want to fix it? Who says I still don't want revenge for my father?"

"You don't." My tone is certain. Something has changed within Lysander, and I think it's everything to do with his destined mate, my Ellelin. "Do you know, at one point in the Crown Race, I was ready to destroy every court to keep her to myself? I didn't want to share her, and I would have fought you."

He looks at me for the first time, a bit of surprise in his green eyes. "You would have betrayed us all for her?"

I don't pause and there isn't a bit of doubt in my voice. "Yes." I glance behind me, seeing Arden shifting into his dragon and making my people scatter like the wind at the sight of the huge fire dragon. Ellelin's laugh reaches me as she climbs onto his back. "Things changed in the camp when I knew that she needed more than me. That she is a princess from a fallen kingdom who will need her. She has enemies after her that would kill her in a heartbeat. I can't protect her on my own, and maybe it was never meant to be that way. Do you believe in fate, in destiny?"

He scoffs. "Of course, but they fuck me over."

I bite back from saying he causes most of the problems himself and not even fate can change this stubborn fucker's mind. "I believe the mighty gods guide us and forgive us. We have mortal souls, capable of making grave mistakes in the name of love. We all fucked up with Ellelin, and yet she is still giving us a chance to right it, while fighting for us."

I glance at the priests who lie near the edges of the Mists, their chants filling the air. Their temples are at the sides of the Mists, almost hidden within them. There are temples in every single court, protected by the mighty dragons, but these are the biggest, grander than others. My court speaks of stories of these temples, how they existed before dragons ever flew the skies. "Come with me a second, friend."

I'm well aware that if the water king doesn't want to come with me, he won't, and I won't force him. I have no interest in fighting him today, not in front of the dead. Lysander stays at my side to my surprise, following me around the Mist into one of the massive temples. Gold-leaved trees sway, even with no breeze, as we walk down the pathway to the temple. The trees are complemented by completely solid gold pillars that hold a massive statue of a dragon above the entrance, its wings stretched into the surrounding Mists.

Candles line everywhere, the flames green, except for a small pathway leading up to an altar in front of our four mighty dragon gods. Their bodies are those of a mortal, two male and two female, but from their shoulders up, they are dragons. Their heads are dragons, as told in our ancient scrolls. Giant wings spread out of their backs, tipping up to make triangle shapes behind them, and at the tips where they meet, a diamond the size of my palm shines bright. The four mighty dragon gods are impressive to look at, to pray to. No one knows where they really came from or even who started this religion, but I'm hoping in this place, we might finally talk of some truths.

"Talk to me, Lysander." When he doesn't say a word, I pick up a match from the altar and light a candle. I would pray for Ellelin, for Emrys and our safety, but I don't think even these gods have the power to help us now. "In this place, anything you say to me, it will be between us. I've told you a truth of mine. Now tell me a truth of yours."

He is quiet for so long, and then he speaks. His voice is thick with an emotion I know all too well. Shame. "I regret what I did to Ellelin and Arden. A part of me regrets it with all of my soul, and another part still hates him because he got it so easy."

Confused, I face him. "What did he get easy?"

"His parents died as heroes, as good people, as people who loved him. Yes, his family was gone, but he didn't have to live through the misery like I did." He leans on a pillar. "My father was brutal and cruel to most people, but not to me. He loved me, and as a child, I saw only that. I wanted him to love me so much that I never got mad, never got upset, never called him out for the tests. He fucked up, but I still loved him. Maybe I'm an idiot for saying that—"

I cut him off. "You're not an idiot for loving someone that hurts you. I've just stood at my mother's funeral, covered in scars from her. My body and soul are scarred from her own madness, the things that led her to it, and I still love her. I will always love my mother. I understand you, and I understand living in grief cannot be easy. My father…when I came back, he was a shadow. Grief swallowed him, spat him out the other side as something that was no longer a dragon king but a wrath on this world."

Lysander's eyes are full of that wrath now. "My mother was like that for years. I looked after my brother, shielded him from it, let him still have light and love and happiness and never allowed myself any of that. I had to be king from an early age, had to deal with the nobles, the royalty, all of it. *Strong*, *cold*, and *empty* were words I embodied. I had my cousins, older than me, breathing down my neck, trying to take my crown and kill me. I had my mother, who was broken. The love of her life was gone. Her mate, as she claimed.

"She's better now…some days. Other days, she is not. Even now, she shuts herself in her room, barely speaking to anybody. Arden, he had support around him. His people love and adore him. They never thought to betray him, not for a second." He lifts his hands. "Half my court betrayed me the minute that Ares walked in." Lysander laughs humourlessly. "Do you know what that feels like? The people I've sacrificed everything for turned their backs on me in a split second and never looked back."

"We wouldn't betray you," I vow. "Your brothers are here if you let us. You are a good king of vile people, but you can fix that. Show the ones who want to change better ways. They don't need to be the way your father taught. Kick out anybody from your court you don't want in it. Surround yourself with loyal, strong Water Court nobles. You're the king, it's your court. Stop blaming Arden because you're jealous of him. Fix it with him or you'll lose Ellelin, and that will break you. Fate has woven us all together, and she has more than one destined mate. She loves him and she's in love with you. I noticed it straight away. That connection between you both. It was like pure fire, ironic from the Water Court king. But if Elle is anything, she is forgiving and kind. Give her a chance to know the real you."

"I've fucked it up too much, Gray," he mutters, rubbing his face. "I don't even know why you're here, trying to make me feel better. You should hate me too."

I walk over and pat his upper arm. He looks at me in shock, a shock that I've willingly touched his arm. "I'm your brother, and family doesn't quit on each other when they mess up. I can't tell you how to fix it, but I know you can, if you try. Let's find our girl. I have an idea where she is, and then we should go and get a beer."

Lysander pushes off the pillar, leaving with me, and I pray once to the gods that they help fix how broken my brother is. Lysander is not evil, despite his desperate attempts to make the world believe he is. I know, with some effort on his part, he can be the best king the Water Court has ever had. His people could adore him.

We leave the empty temple, walking past the trees, which sing their own song into the wind, a whistle that only shifters can hear. Lysander shifts first, his brilliant blue dragon bursting out of him and jumping into the air. Shifting, for me, is the only time I feel free in my own body. My dragon roars loud, flooding my mind with the strongest of my wants and desires—Ellelin. We soar together through the mountains of my court, around the familiar peaks and shallow rivers. Lysander stays close, following me back to the main city, where I know Ellelin would be. After hours and hours with her in our secret place, she asked to see more of the city. I took her into the city to show her around, and my people bowed to her as their queen. She might not be crowned yet, but she is my queen. End of story.

Lysander lands next to me on a grassy ledge on the far right side of the city. "Flying around here never fails to make my dragon happy. You have many rivers."

I chuckle low. "My dragon doesn't feel the same in your court. Too much water."

He grins at me for a second before following me through the thick gates of the city. I pick up Ellelin's sweet scent in the air, like a drug tugging me in, and I can't do anything but follow until I find her. My dragon is obsessed, almost more than I am, and if we don't see her, then he will be pissed with me.

Lysander frowns at the countryside on the outskirts of the city, the rolling green hills and stable farms scattered about. The pyramids cast deep shadows around the greens, but the light pours in from outside, from gaps in the mountain designed by our engineers to maximise the brightness in here. A small farm lies in the distance, which I showed her only last night, and I know she is there. "Where are we? Ellelin is near, but why would she come here?"

"To show Arden her new favourite part of the Earth Court," I answer. I remember her face last night, how all of her lit up with joy. Lysander frowns at me, but curiosity lights his eyes up. We walk up to the barn, and it's pretty much deserted of any caretakers, which is just as well, considering the noises coming from the barn. I'm not too surprised to find Arden and Ellelin together. He's kissing her, pressing her against the wall, his hand cupping her breast under her shirt. His groans echo around the barn, mixed with hers, and if they are aware we are watching, they don't show it, as they don't stop.

I love that they don't stop. Lysander goes still with fury, whereas I have a completely different reaction to him touching her, holding her, tearing at her clothes. My blood heats and my cock hardens.

Lysander swears, turning and walking away, only to smack right into a Scalis, who neighs in displeasure.

The Scalis race, a specialty breed of horses, are native only to my court, and I'm not sure Lysander has even seen one before. They began as regular horses, but now they are far more special than that and they have their own magic. Instead of fur, the Scalis are completely covered in scales. This one has green scales, the same colour as Lysander's eyes, and it neighs loudly, stomping its hoof on the ground. The eyes of the Scalis are burning green flames within darkness, and each is born with only those eyes in common. "I've heard of these but never seen one. I can see why my mate is enchanted with this court."

"They can run faster, faster than any creature in Ayiolyn," I boast. I'm proud of my court, and the Scalis are one of our treasures. "My grandfather once speculated that they might be able to run fast enough to stop time. Never tested that theory, but we have solely focused on breeding for the last fifty years. We finally have a strong herd."

Lysander runs his hand through the mane of the horse, the rows of little scales clinking. "We have horses made of water in my court, but these are something special. Any chance I could buy a few from you?"

A neigh fills the air and I pat my brother's back. "You only want one to impress her." He smirks at me, but the emptiness doesn't leave his eyes. "At some point, you have to accept that people love you, even if you're an asshole, even if you've fucked up a countless number of times. You should speak to your mother about it. About all of it. Tell her your truth, and then we'll all be able to move on as a family."

Lysander shrugs my hand off his shoulder, walking away before he shifts into his dragon, blue scales glittering across the sky before he flies out. He still isn't having one of my horses.

CHAPTER 14

*D*awn barely crests outside of the balcony as Lysander and Arden watch the Earth Court with me. Grayson walks out to us, nodding at Arden and Lysander, who stand apart like they might permanently be if I can't find a way to fix this all. Arden strokes my arm. "You look tired. Are you sure you're ready for this?"

"We can wait," Lysander suggests, a dark promise lying in his words. He has avoided all the times I've tried to speak to him alone, and I'm not sure what I'd say anyway. Grayson told me he spoke to Lysander, but he didn't say much more. I don't have to answer, he knows what I would say. Emrys cannot wait. I will not leave him there. My air king needs me. "Then we fight, one more time."

Grayson makes a portal, shimmering water like a veil, burning to life in front of us all. In between Lysander and Arden, I follow Grayson through the portal and out into the Air Court. The throne room of the Air Court is on a giant flat rock, floating in the middle of the blue sky. There is nothing and no one for as far as I can see. Aphrodite and Ares are sitting on a half-circle throne made of white onyx, and it is massive, as tall as a house. There are several rows of seats on either side of a white stone pathway that leads to the throne. The rock spreads out far, but I'm confused about where the rest of the court is. Arden leans down, whispering to me. "The cities are underneath, hidden in the clouds. Flying is the only way between them."

Lysander's hand brushes mine, on purpose, as we walk down the path to the throne. I link our pinkie fingers for a second, just to tell him I'm here, before letting go. My heart races when I finally see Emrys. He looks worse than he did a few days ago. Paler, weaker, thinner. I know they said they wouldn't hurt him, but looking after him, perhaps that was not part of it. I blow out a breath of cold air as we finish our walk, standing before the gods, who are not welcome in our world. Aphrodite doesn't look impressed now; she's not laughing or smiling anymore. In fact, she looks downright pissed off. "You didn't expect me to win three of your tests, did you?"

"Maybe I underestimated the granddaughter of Hera. I knew your grandmother an age ago. You're smarter than I gave you credit for," she claims, leaning her head on her hand, her long hair flowing around the onyx. "I always believe love wins, but I am the goddess of love, so I will win this. You will not prevail in this. Not without a great price."

Grayson's voice is like death. "Is that the word of a god, or someone desperate?"

She doesn't answer him. Her eyes flash with anger for a second. She lifts her hand, and Emrys stands. "This one is my favourite, so handsome and strong. I saved him for the best idea." My stomach feels like it's full of lead as I try to ignore her. "The test is for you and Emrys alone, and you are not dressed accordingly to fight in it." Her magic sweeps around me, every inch of my skin it touches feeling like it is being stung by lightning before it fades, leaving me in a long purple ball gown.

I'm suddenly pitched into darkness, feeling Lysander and Arden grabbing for my arms. Then they are gone. I fall, gasping in the icy air, before landing on a hard surface with a thump that shakes my ribs. I scream on impact, feeling like my shoulders dislodged from the fall as pain shoots through, down my chest. I groan, rolling on my back and trying to look around, but I can't see anything. She's blinded me. I trip over the layers of the dress as I stand, bits of it ripping, and my bare feet get cut on sharp stone.

It wasn't that dark before, and even if it was that dark in here, I think I could see something at least. I reach out into thin air, but there's nothing, and the dress makes it impossible to move far without tripping on it. "Emrys!" I scream his name, but only the wind answers me, echoing loud and howling away. My voice echoes like I'm in a cave, but it's so cold here, too windy to be a cave. Suddenly something cold rests in my hand. A key, from the feel of it.

Aphrodite's voice fills my ear. "Follow the air, trust your instincts, and unlock the cage before he stops breathing. He won't be able to breathe for long, and if one dies, so does your world."

Fear slinks into my chest as her voice disappears, and I scream, reaching in the air for her, for anything solid. I take a few steps forward before stopping, feeling like I'm about to stand on something that tips off the edge. I trace the edge with the tip of my feet, knowing I can't go that way. I spin backwards, walking a few steps until I slam against a smooth, cool wall. Turning, I put my back against it and suck in a deep breath. I need to calm myself down. Breathe and focus. Emrys needs me.

"I'm here," Lysander whispers into my mind, and I can feel Arden there too. "Grayson is with us. What's wrong? What is going on?"

"She's blinded me and it's hard to breathe here. She gave me a key and told me to find Emrys before he runs out of air," I reply, unable to hide my panic. What if I don't find him in time?

"You must be in the cages below the throne room. It's a place where people are taken who have betrayed the court," Arden explains. "The air pressure is low there, and there are cages that slowly drain the rest of the air out until…" He pauses. "You need to move, Elle. Find him."

"I know, but I can't see!" I shout back. "She seems to have a real thing about these kinds of places. Why exactly do you have them again?"

Lysander fills my mind like water, the sheer opposite to Arden's fire. "Calm, Elle. Focus. It's a cage with a series of locks, but the top one opens it. It's not a maze, it should be quite straightforward to find your way. Small steps. Terrin claimed Emrys was your mate too, right?"

"Yes," I whisper, moving across the wall, clinging to it like it might save me from suddenly falling off. The dress blows around my legs in the breeze, the soft fabric clinging to me.

"I could always find you. I could always sense you near," Lysander tells me.

"Same. Your existence was a mirror to my own, even without the bond in place," Arden agrees with Lysander. "Trust yourself and find him."

Easier said than done. They aren't blind, in a place that hurts to breathe, walking a ledge. "What if I fall?"

"You won't," Lysander vows. The trust between us all falls like ashes from a fire, slow and steady. "We trust you. We know you—"

The wind howls and whips around me, and every breath burns my throat, my lungs. Silence. I can't hear them anymore. Our connection is just gone. Aphrodite must have figured out a way to cut them off from me. Emrys needs me.

I can find him. If anyone can find him, it's me. Emrys, who reads books and holds me when I'm scared. Emrys, who took me flying, made me laugh in my worst moments, and is always there for me with no questions asked. Emrys, the kindest dragon shifter king. He can't die in this place, waiting for me. I close my eyes and try to feel for him, feel for that part of me that loves him. I scream in frustration when nothing happens. I can't make it snap into place. "For fuck's sake, someone help me! Gods, someone needs to help me!"

My scream isn't answered, and any bit of panic I tried to bury comes rushing to the surface. If I don't move, he's going to die. If I move, there's a very good chance I die. I already know my answer as my foot steps forward. Dying is better than doing nothing and being a coward. I'm Princess fucking Ellelin of the mighty Spirit Court, and I will not be a coward.

Every step makes my body shake, and I keep moving, careful not to step off the end of the ledge. Every step feels wobbly on the gritty rock as I walk forward, hoping and praying I'm going the right way by just following my instincts. Everything is just one giant pit of air and rock walls. I keep breathing in and out. It's so cold. My skin is prickling all over. The gown isn't keeping me warm in this place. The Air Court is my least favourite, I've decided.

I walk straight forward, hoping and praying that

I'm going to find this cage, knowing his time is running out. I turn around a corner where the whistling wind sounds less strong, and I swear I almost hear Emrys. My heart pounds. "Emrys?"

I'm sure it was him. He shouted at me. I might be going mad, it might not be him, but I keep walking forward, faster this time. Faster even when I know there's a chance I could slip straight off into the air. "Ellelin!" Emrys whispers, sounding louder this time, and hope makes my body feel on fire. He sounds breathless, like there isn't much time left.

I slam face-first into some thick metal bars, and I wince, tasting blood in my mouth. "Emrys, is that you? I'm coming, I have a key!"

"Ellelin, you're really here," he manages to say. "Unlock the cage at the top."

I search for the lock, reaching as high as I can get on my tiptoes. "Where's the latch?" I say more to myself, and Emrys doesn't answer me. My fingertips just about touch the door lock, and I lift the key, trying to push it in. I realise it needs to be upside down, and I turn it, finally getting the key in. With a click, the door opens and my vision comes back as I fall through the cage, right in front of Emrys. My Emrys, the handsome, kind air king, who took me flying above the castle when I felt trapped in a cage. Emrys, who stole my heart so easily, with words and protection he so effortlessly gave me. Emrys…who I didn't get to in time. The world stops, slowing to a whistle in the wind, as I see Emrys on the ground, completely unconscious. Still, like a frozen statue of a mighty king. "No!" I scream. I feel nothing but pure dread sink straight into my soul, sickness rising in my throat as I rush to him. I roll him onto his back, watching his chest for a second. He's not breathing.

HIS CHEST ISN'T MOVING. HE ISN'T BREATHING. NO. NO. NO. NO. NOT HIM. NOT ONE OF MY DRAGON KINGS.

"Emrys!" I scream, jumping on him and starting CPR. I don't even know how to do it right; I failed the class at school, but I have to try something. I push down on his chest again and again, hoping it's enough. Tears fall down my face, dropping into his pale face as time slips by, no matter how much I beg for it to stop. "Emrys. Emrys, please no. Emrys, don't you dare die on me. I can't…please don't die. Don't die!" I scream, my powers returning in a wave. My shadow dragon forms under Emrys and me, lifting us both up in the air. "Lysander. I have to get to Lysander. He can heal him."

I command my shadow dragon to fly above, out

of the prison, breaking it apart with my shadows. We fly up in the air and around the rock before landing back in the Air Court throne room. I leave Emrys's body in a pool of shadows as I stand up. "Lysander!"

My scream just echoes, and I realise I can't feel him nearby. He's far away, but I can't sense where. Too far. I reach for Emrys, ready to make a portal out of here and to the Water Court for someone to heal him, when Aphrodite's laugh reaches me and her red magic wraps around me, launching me across the throne room and dumping me on the stone in front of her. She laughs at me. "You failed the test, and your heart is breaking. So sad."

"No, I didn't!" I scream, crawling to my feet. "He is not dead."

She waves a hand at me, rising. "It doesn't matter. We only needed to go to each court to retrieve something to open portals to every world." She looks to the side where Ares is waiting with the staff. The top of the staff has four crystals on it, one for each court, and they are glowing. I wipe my tears away. "What is that?"

Ares spins it. "It will open a portal to a world we've wanted to return to for a while, where the gods were born. Lapetus. Where wolves think they're gods. Where the gods bound themselves, their souls, to wolf shifters to try to live forever. We don't have any intention of doing that, but ruling what is left of that world would be better than ruling the carcasses of here. We'll come back, of course, when we have more power."

Ares slams his power straight at me. The test doesn't protect me this time, but my shadows come up in a wall, pushing his magic to the side. He's strong, knocking me back a few steps and pushing on the limit of my power. I look behind me at Emrys, who is still not moving. He can't be dead. I refuse to believe it. A portal opens to the side, and Arty steps out. Her eyes widen as she looks at us all. "Stop, mother, father. That's enough. Just go to your world and don't come back."

"Where are they?" I demand.

"Haven't you lost enough?" Aphrodite questions. "We tested the staff with your kings. You could say they are not in this world anymore. I left you the air king, but that's a shame. Dead king."

"He's not gone!" I scream at her. "He's not." I desperately look at Arty, who is near Emrys. "Get him to the Water Court. GO!"

"She won't," Aphrodite coos. "She isn't powerful enough to make a portal. She used a drop of my magic left in a device to make a one-way portal here."

Hopelessness threatens to sink me onto my knees. "Love is delusional, just like you are, my daughter. Come with us to this world, and we will forgive you."

Arty sinks to her knees next to Emrys and takes his hand. "I'd rather stay here and die with my friends if that is what fate wishes."

Ares starts making a portal, nothing like I've ever seen before. Green spiralling magic in strange patterns bursts into the air, spitting green embers in every direction. They're going to go to another world. They're going to go and try to destroy another world. I run at them, knowing I can't let them do that. I must stop them. Aphrodite slips in front of me, red magic exploding into the air, but my shadows cut through it as I pull my daggers out of the shadows and head straight for Ares. He's the one that needs to die first. He took everything from me. My father…my court. Everything.

I run straight for him with the daggers, and the staff drops to the floor by the portal that is half open with a thud. He grabs my wrists, stopping me, knocking one of the daggers out of my hands, and it clangs onto the stone. Screaming, I push the other between us, and he uses all his magic in his hands to push against me and my shadows powering me. "You will die for this, princess. Do you think my wife will let you kill me? She's going to kill this court and you, then we'll leave this world. You should have died all those years ago. I should never have let you escape."

"You *never* let me escape. My father made sure I escaped. The Spirit Court made sure I'd escape so I'd come back and destroy you." I see Aphrodite coming for us in the distance, bitter anger written all over her face. I have to kill him before she gets here. Pulling all the power I can, I push at the dagger between us, cutting through his hands. He slams power into my arms, and one of my wrists snaps. I scream, accidentally dropping the dagger, and he grabs my wrist, leeching my power. I literally feel my power draining from me to him. As his eyes brighten, he laughs and laughs as I fall in his grip, weakness hitting me like a wave.

"No…"

"You're weak and alone, princess," Ares sneers at me.

"She is not alone." Suddenly, one of my daggers plunges straight through Ares chest, through his heart, and his blood sprays across my cheek. My eyes widen as Emrys steps up from behind Ares, weak but standing. He uses his air powers to make the dagger go through his chest. Another one of my daggers lifts out of the air and cuts through his chest on the other side, impaling him completely. I hear Ares choke as he lets me go.

I glare up at him. "Those daggers are blessed by the god of nightmares and horror. They are alive, and the souls in them are worse than any evil you've met. They'll destroy anything they touch with the most unimaginable pain as they claw you apart. A present from my uncle. Now go to hell and beg Hades not to curse your soul."

"This is for the Spirit Court. This is for all the courts," Emrys whispers to him. "There will be peace in this world when you've gone, and no one will remember you."

Aphrodite screams as Ares roars in pain and collapses, dead. Aphrodite runs through the portal that Ares opened, and it blinks out of existence right after her. I grin, wrapping my arms around Emrys's neck, leaning back to kiss him. He looks pale as I hug him again, needing a moment to know he is okay, and I glance at Arty, who is pale and on her knees, looking at her hands. She saved him. I don't know how, but she did, and Emrys then killed her father. Ares's staff catches my eye where it lies on the ground behind his dead body. It might be over in this world, but my other dragon kings and Aphrodite are in another world of wolf shifters… and I have to go after them.

EPILOGUE

ELVI ILROTH, QUEEN OF THE SPIRIT COURT

The world is real, warm, and brighter than it's been for so many years. The damp, dim dungeons I've called home for thousands of days, with only Ares as company, are gone. Instead, I can smell laundry, flowers, and embers of a fire. A soft, gentle hand strokes my cheek, and a woman is humming a familiar song I remember from my childhood. I'd know this small, cosy room anywhere. It was my home, from my childhood, a place I thought I'd never get to see again. The woman keeps singing, lulling me back from the spell, from the magic latched around my soul like a chain.

I sang the same song to my baby, but she always

preferred the haunting music of the song of the fifth court, a song made of shadows and darkness. A song which the castle knew was made for her. I remember the day she was born, almost like it was only yesterday. It was such a long labour, over four days, and by the end, I thought time would end before she came into the world. Then she was there, pink and screaming her lungs off, telling the Spirit Court they had a new ruler. The castle played the song over and over as I touched her sweet face, gazed into her eyes, and watched her father fall in love in a heartbeat. It was the single greatest day of my entire life. It is the memory I sink into when I need strength, a comfort for me. I promised that day to protect her forever, to be her watcher, to be the hand on her shoulder, guiding her through her darkest days…but Ares stole that promise and crushed it.

I saw her. My Ellelin. She is so grown up, a woman now, and she is the image of her father. Her hair was once as black as ravens' wings, but now it's the deepest purple that reminds me of a twilight sunset in the Fire Court…but she was hurt. I couldn't help her. I couldn't stop him.

"Ellelin?" I gasp, my voice cracking with every word, like talking is forbidden to me now.

My husband is gone. Dead. The court is destroyed, and I'm…where am I?

"Oh, thank the skies and heavens. You're awake. The spell worked. I thought I might have to sacrifice some humans or even the cursed cat to wake you," my mother exclaims in relief, and a strange cat meows in protest, its bell ringing as it runs away.

My mother, Hera, is here. It feels like just yesterday I begged the castle to open a portal and send Ellelin to my mother. I knew she would keep her safe, bring her up with love, and teach her to fight. I kissed my husband goodbye for the last time and vowed to protect his child with every inch of magic I had left. We both gave up everything to stop Ares, protect our people, and give Ellelin a real chance at a life. "Where is she? Where is my daughter?"

"Calm down, Elvi. Breathe," my mother commands, her voice sharp as a knife. I widen my eyes, pushing off the thin blanket, searching for my powers only to find nothing. Ares might not have me in his grasp, but he took my powers. He made sure I wouldn't be able to escape. Locking him down there took everything from me.

Anger fuels me as I face my mother. "Where is my daughter?"

She sighs, picking up my thin hand and patting it. "Ellelin is strong, powerful, and able to fight her own battles. I trained her myself, loved her like my own. Phobos taught her to defend herself, and I taught her magic. She's…okay."

"My Ellelin will never be safe so long as there are gods in Ayiolyn," I snap, and my mother winces. My shoulders drop. "I'm sorry, Mother. Thank you for loving her, for teaching her to fight… I just need to see my daughter."

My mother cups my cheek. "I know the feeling. I thought you were lost to me… I could not sense your soul in this world or any."

"I did what was needed," I hoarsely whisper. "And paid for it. Ellelin…let's go to her."

"We can't." My mother shakes her head. "She's gone after Ares and Aphrodite to save the other court kings. There is much I need…"

The rest of her words blur away as pure terror lances through my chest. "She can't kill him! No one can! We have to stop her!" I scramble to my feet. "NOW!"

"Calm down," my mother gently coaxes me, touching my hands.

"No, you don't understand why I've been trapped for so many years with him. We didn't kill him for a reason," I all but shout at her, like she might be able to warn my daughter. "We found out something during our research on the gods. My king, he knew Ares would come for us, so he searched every court, every inch of our world for a way to kill him, and that's when he found out the truth. He cannot be killed. It's why we did everything back then, why I used the last of my magic to lock him in the castle with me. That's why we trapped him. *He can't be killed*. Ares can't be killed, not by anybody. The person who kills Ares will become Ares, and he will take their power. He transports himself from body to body like that, absorbing power as he goes." My mother's eyes widen, fear flashing in the depths. "If Ellelin kills him, she will become him, and he will get the power of the Spirit Court like he always wanted. There is nothing in this world that would be able to save her!"

My mother looks out the window, her tanned skin draining of colour. The night sky is bright with a thousand stars, but one is faded. I felt it too, the shake felt across all worlds as I woke and he died. A feeling the stars themselves share across the worlds. A god has been killed.

Keep reading with Court of Dragons and Ruin here...

AFTERWORD

Thank you for reading! For those who guessed from the hints throughout this book, this is in the same world as Fall Mountain Shifters (Her Wolves) and there will be major crossovers in the next book. There are five books planned in this series and the next is on pre-order now. Link here. This one is called Court of Dragons and Ruin.

This book, like all my others, is for my family and for my readers.

About G. Bailey

G. Bailey is a USA Today and international bestselling author of books that are filled with everything from dragons to pirates. Plus, fantasy worlds and breath-taking adventures. G. Bailey is from England and loves rainy days with her family.

(You can find exclusive teasers, random giveaways, and sneak peeks of new books on the way in Bailey's Pack on Facebook or on TikTok— gbaileybooks)

Find more books by G. Bailey on Amazon...
Link here.

More Books by G. Bailey

Her Guardians Series

Her Fate Series

Protected By Dragons Series

Lost Time Academy Series

The Demon Academy Series

Dark Angel Academy Series

Shadowborn Academy Series

Dark Fae Paranormal Prison Series

Saved By Pirates Series

The Marked Series

Holly Oak Academy Series

The Alpha Brothers Series

A Demon's Fall Series

The Familiar Empire Series

From The Stars Series

The Forest Pack Series

The Secret Gods Prison Series

The Rejected Mate Series

Fall Mountain Shifters Series

Royal Reapers Academy Series

The Everlasting Curse Series

The Moon Alpha Series

The Dragon Crown Series

Chrysalis Pack Series

PART I
BONUS READ OF HEIR OF MONSTERS

BONUS READ OF HEIR OF MONSTERS

A monster has stalked me my entire life.

But now I'm hunting him.

My job is to hunt monsters, and I'm damn good at it —until a monster breaks into my apartment in the middle of the night and kidnaps me.

Turns out he isn't just a monster.

He's the Wyern King.

Wyerns, a race feared by everyone, are known to be stronger than the fae who rule my world, and no one has seen them in years until now.

The king needs my help to track down his missing sister from within a city his race is banished from, and I'm the best he can find.

Only, he isn't the only one looking for monsters in Ethereal City.

The Fae Queen's grandson is missing.

Working for fae, monster or not, is risky. Most who are hired end up dead, and I have too much to lose to end up as one of them.

I'm going to find the missing royals and be careful about it, especially with my grumpy boss breathing down my neck and watching my every move.

The Wyern King is cruel, cold, and unbelievably beautiful for a male… and my new enemy.

Heir of Monsters is a full-length paranormal Monster Romance with mature themes. This is a spicy enemies-to-lovers romance and is recommended for 17+.

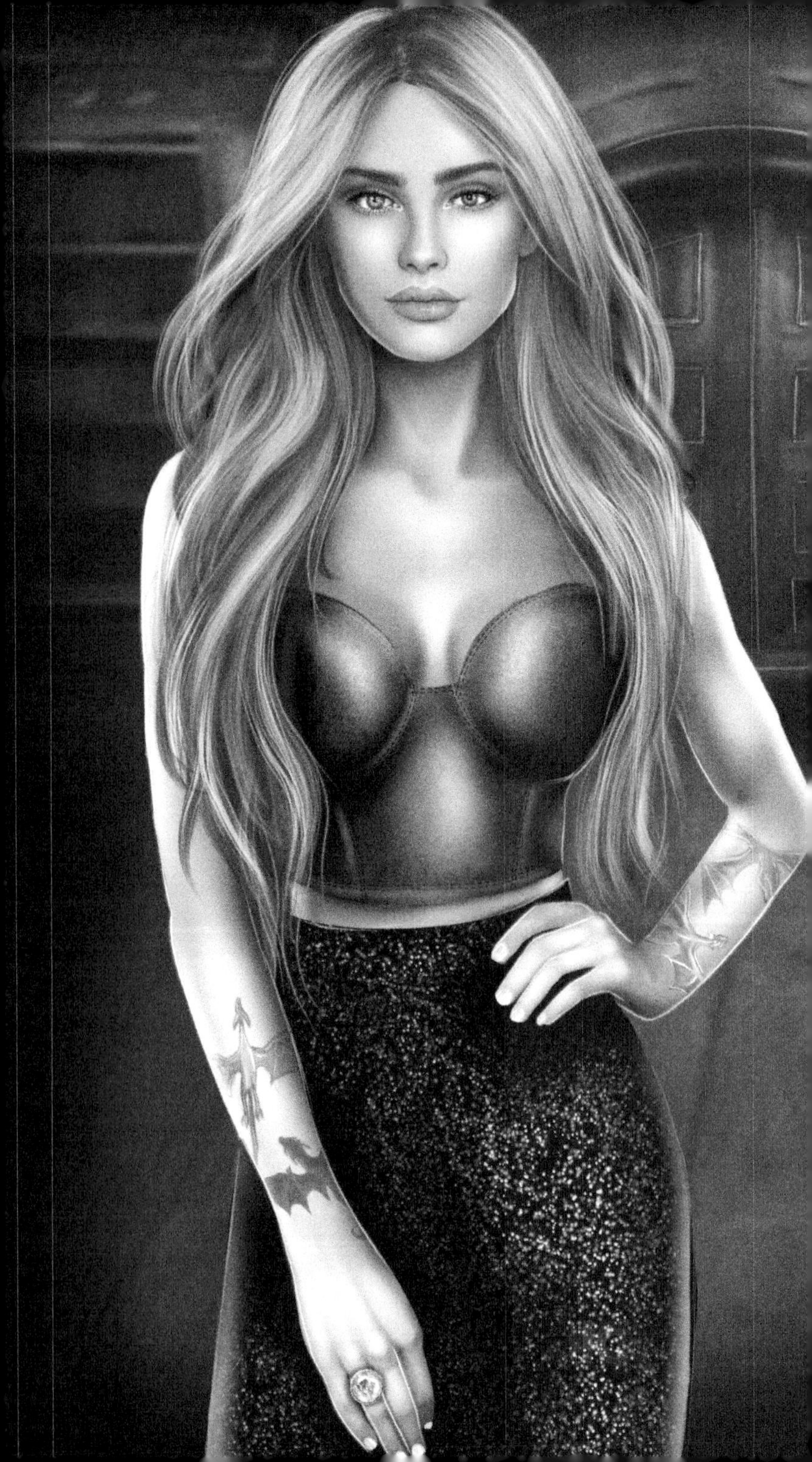

BONUS READ OF HEIR OF MONSTERS

Monsters are real.

If I needed any more proof than the thing in front of me, then I might be the one going mad in this world. The monster twists its grotesque head back to me, assessing me with its red eyes and mottled skin. It stands at over seven feet, two feet taller than me, and its once mortal-like body is a mixture of wolf and gods know what else. I risk taking my eyes off it for a second to look for my partner, and I catch a flash of red in the darkness behind the monster. I block out the awful stench of the creature and the rattling noise of its bones as it moves while I look for a safe way to take it down without getting us killed.

Clenching my magically blessed dagger in my

hand, I whistle loudly. The monster roars loud enough to shake the derelict walls of the ruins before barrelling for me, each step shaking the ground. Like the dumbass that I am, I don't run but charge right back at it to meet it halfway. This plan better work, or I'm so fired. Or dead. I'm not sure which is worse.

"Calliophe! To your left!"

I barely hear my partner's warning shout before something hard rams into the side of me, shooting me into the air. I crash into the stone wall, all the air leaving my lungs as I roll to the floor and gasp in pain.

That hurt.

Blood fills my mouth as I push myself up and pause as I get a look at the giant cat-like thing in front of me. It might have once been a cat, even an exotic and expensive breed, but now it's been warped and changed like the monster behind it. It might even have been his pet. Once.

It lunges for me, snapping a row of sharp yellow teeth, and I narrowly jump to the side before kicking it with my boot. It hisses as I grapple for my dagger in the dust and slash the air between us as a warning as I crouch down. Its eyes are like yellow puddles of water, and I can see my reflection.

Despite being covered in dust and dirt, my pink eyes glow slightly, and I look tiny in comparison. Even tiny, with a dagger, can be deadly. If the main monster runs, we might not get another chance to catch it for days, so I call to it, "Over here!"

The strange cat hisses once more, and the hair on its back rises. It straightens with its five strange legs that make it almost as tall as a dog.

A pain-filled female grunt echoes to me, and I clench my teeth. "I need a little help over here, Calli! Or I'm singing and screwing us both over!"

Dammit. I'm going to be the one buying the drinks tonight if she sings. Or worse, explaining this messed up mission to our boss. I'd rather buy the whole entire bar drinks and be poor. I jump on the cat, surprising it and slamming my dagger into its throat as it scratches and bites me before it goes still in my arms. I gently lower it to the ground, closing my eyes for a moment. I love animals, but whatever that was, death was a mercy for it. I pull my dagger out of it, yellow sticky blood dripping down my hand as I run across the ruins to Nerelyth. Somehow, she has gotten herself under a large piece of stone barely propped against a wall where she's hiding, and the monster is on top of it, clawing at the gap and nearly squishing her. I see her wave her arm at me from the small gap, and I sigh. There is only one way to capture a monster. Get up close and personal, and hope it doesn't eat me.

Thankfully, with Nerelyth's distraction, the monster's back is to me as I pull out my enchanted rope and let it wrap around my leg as I run across the ruins and close the gap between us, keeping my footsteps silent. Nerelyth's eyes widen when she spots me, but I don't pause as I leap off a fallen ledge and land on the creature's back, grunting at the impact on my swollen ribs, but my dagger easily slides into its back. Its skin is like goo, and I struggle to hold on as it straightens with a roar, but I lasso my rope around its neck with my other hand. The monster almost screams like a mortal as I let go, sliding down the monster's back and landing in a heap on the ground. I crawl backwards as the rope magically wraps itself over and over around the monster until it ties its legs together and it falls to the side. The rope won't kill it, but it will stay locked up like this for hours, depending on how good the enchantment is.

With a grunt, I stand up and wipe the goo off my hands and walk over to where Nerelyth is still hiding. I tilt my head and look down at my partner, who has her eyes closed. "It's sorted now."

Nerelyth is lying face up under the stone, her red hair splayed around her. Her chest is moving fast as she finally opens her eyes and looks over at me, arching an eyebrow. "Thank you. Again," I tell her. "We might have fucked up." I offer her my hand as she brushes the dust off her leather clothes. "Any chance you love me for saving you and you will explain it to the boss?"

"Not a chance," she chuckles as I help her climb out, light shining in from the bright sun hanging over us. We both stop to look over at the monster, who is trying to escape the rope. "Third one this month. Where do you think they are coming from?"

"Not a clue," I mutter, eyeing the monster suspiciously. "I'm not sure M.A.D. even knows where the hybrids are coming from. They still happily send us out with no warning that this wasn't a normal job. Assholes."

She shrugs a slender shoulder, picking out flecks of dust from her flawless waist-length dark red hair that matches the red curls of water marks around her cheek that go all the way down her neck to her back. I'm certain I look much worse than she does, and I'm not even attempting to take my hair out of my braid to fix it. "The money is worth it."

Lie. I've been in the Monster Acquisitions Division, aka M.A.D., for three years, and the pay has never been good compared to the other divisions, and we both know it. Like everyone says, you have to be literally mad to make it in M.A.D. for more than a month.

Most enforcers, like us, are sent here as a punishment for fucking up. I had no choice but to take this job, as it was all I could get with my background, lack of money, and young age when I started at only eighteen. I glance at my partner of just one year and wonder again why a siren is working in one of the shittiest divisions in Ethereal City. Sirens are one of the wealthiest races, and the few I know work at the top of the enforcers. Not at the bottom, like us, which makes me question my friend's motives for being here with me once again. "Drinks tonight?"

"You know it," she says with a friendly smile and tired viridescent green eyes. "I'll send a Flame to get some enforcers down here to take him in. You get back to the office and good luck."

I groan and send a silent prayer to the dragon goddess herself to save me.

* * *

I HEAD across the busy market street and look up at the Enforcer Headquarters as I stand on the sidewalk. The streets around me are filled with mortals and supernaturals heading to or from the bustle of the market to buy wares, food or nearly anything they want. The market hill is right at the top of the city, and it's the biggest market in Ethereal City. Fae horses wait by their owners' carts at the side of the main path, and I eye a soft white horse nearby for a moment and admire its shiny coat.

From this point, I can see nearly all of Ethereal City, from the elaborate seven hundred and four skyscrapers right down to the emerald green sea and the circular bay at the bottom of the city. Ethereal City was created over two thousand years ago, and the bay is even older than that. Dozens, if not hundreds, of ships line the ports, and they look like sparkling silver lines on the crystal green sea. Beyond that, the swirling seas of the largest lake in the world stretch all the way to the horizon and far beyond.

Most of Wyvcelm is this land, wrapped around the jeweled seas between Ethereal City and Goldway City on the other side. There are a few islands off the mainland, and one of them I want to go to one day—when I'm rich enough. Junepit City, the pleasure lands. I shake my head, pushing away that dream to focus on the Jeweled Seas, and I think of Nerelyth every time I see it.

The Jeweled Seas are ruled by the Siren King, and no one ever travels through them unless you are a siren, escorted by sirens, or want to die. Nerelyth told me once about how going through the fast, creature-filled rapids and the narrow cliff channels makes it nearly impossible to survive for long unless you know the way and can control the water. Above the sea level is worse as enchanted tornadoes reach high into the sky, swirling constantly over the waters controlled by the sirens themselves. That's why they're one of the richest races in Wyvcelm, because if the sirens didn't control the tornadoes, they would rip into both Ethereal City and Goldway City, ending thousands of lives. But they are not richer than the fae who rule over our lands and pay them to keep us safe.

I turn to my right, looking up at the castle that looms above the entire city. Its black spiraling towers, shining slate roofs and shimmering silver windows make it stand out anywhere that I am in the city. It was made that way, to make sure we always know who is ruling us. The immortal Fae Queen. Our queen lives in that palace and has done her entire immortal life. Thousands of years, if the history books are right and our longest reigning queen to date. She keeps us safe from the dangers outside the walls of the city, from the Wyern King and his clan of Wyerns who live over in the Forgotten Lands. They are the true monsters of our world.

A cold, salty breeze blows around me, and I shiver as I pull myself from my thoughts and look back up at the building where I go every single day. The Enforcer Headquarters, one of twelve in the city, and they all look the exact same. Symmetrical pillars line the outline of the two-story building that stretches far back. Perfectly trimmed bushes make a square around the bottom floor, and three staircases lead up to the platform outside the enormous main door. All of it is black, from the stone to the bushes, except for the white door, which is always open and always guarded by new junior enforcers. I walk up the hundred and fifty-two steps to the doors, and both the enforcers nod at me, letting me in without needing to check my I.D. I'm sure they have heard of me—and not in a good way. My list of fuckups is a mile long.

I glance at the young enforcer, a woman with cherry red lipstick and black hair, and wonder why she chose to sign up to be an enforcer. I doubt she was like me, fresh out of the foster system and left with no other decent options but this. Many don't want this job, and with the right schooling, they don't have to take it. It's hard work and long hours... and we die a lot. I've been lucky to skirt death myself a few times, and each time, I thank the dragon goddess for saving me. I smile at the junior enforcer and walk into the building, across the shiny black marble floors and up to the receptionist, Wendy, who sits behind a wall of glass and a small, tidy oak desk. I like Wendy, who is part witch, but I don't hold that against her. Her black hair is curled up and pinned into a bun, and she is wearing a long blue skirt and a white chemise top. "Hello, Calliophe. I missed you yesterday during the quarter term meeting."

"Sorry about that. Monster hunting and all," I say with a genuine smile even if I'm not sorry at all for missing another boring meeting. "Is he in there?"

She nods at the steps by the side of her office that lead up to the only full floor office on the top level. All the rest of us have our offices below his. The boss made sure that he had the only room above when he was transferred here a year ago. Her dark, nearly black eyes flicker nervously. "Upstairs. He's not in a great mood tonight."

"Brilliant," I tightly say and take a deep breath. "Thanks, Wendy. See you around if I survive the boss's bad mood."

"Good luck," she whispers to me before I walk to the stairs and head up to the top level. I'm glad I took the time to quickly get changed into a black tank top and high-waisted black jeans. My pink hair flows around my shoulders to the middle of my back, reminding me that I need a haircut soon.

When I get to the top of the stairs, I pause to look over the gigantic space that I'm rarely invited into, noticing how it smells like him. Masculine, minty and cool, which suits the space he has claimed. Massive floor-to-ceiling windows stretch across the back area, giving magnificent views of the fae castle upon the hill and the rest of the city below it. The towers, the small buildings, the people are easy to see from this vantage point. The sun slowly sets off in the distance, casting cascades of mandarin, lemony yellow and scarlet red light across the tips of buildings and across the shiny black floor. The light spreads across my boots as I walk into the room and finally look over at him. He is sitting at his desk, the single piece of furniture in this whole massive space, and on the desk is a Flame.

Flames are small red gnomes that use flames to travel from one place to another, and in general, are useful pests. The city is full of them, and for a coin, they will send a message for you. I've heard that you can ask the Flames to send anything you want, even death, to another, but it comes with a price only the dragon goddess herself could bear. They are ancient creatures and not to be messed with. I wouldn't dare ask for more than a message, and not many would. The Flame looks back at me with its soulless black eyes, and then he disappears in a flicker of flames, leaving embers bouncing across the desk.

Merrick looks up at me with his gorgeous dark grey eyes, and the room becomes tense. Some would say his eyes are colorless, but I don't think that's true. His eyes are a perfect reflection of any color in the room, and there are others that claim his grey eyes suggest he has angelic blood. Which is laughable. The Angelic Children, a race so rare we hardly ever see them, are said to be endlessly kind.

There's nothing nice or kind about Merrick Night. My boss. His dark brown hair is perfectly gelled into place, not a stray daring to be wrong, and it's much like the expensive black suit, the perfect black tie, flawless white shirt tucked into black trousers he wears, all of it expensive. He doesn't wear the enforcer leathers, magically made material, and he has never explained why.

I stop before his desk and cross my arms.

"Do you want to explain yourself, or should I start, Miss Sprite?"

His deep, cocky, arrogant voice irritates me as we both know he knows what happened and why. But fine, if we are going to play this game.

I resist the urge to glower at my boss, not wanting to get fired, as I lift my chin. "I'll start, boss. We were told it was a simple monster on the loose on the left side of the city—Yenrtic District. It was suggested that an exiled werewolf had murdered mortals, and they called us to take him in. That was all that we were told, and we went to hunt him as per our job. He might have been part werewolf once, but he wasn't anymore when we found him. He was a hybrid, twisted and changed into something indescribable, but I'm sure we can go take a visit if you wish to see it."

"That won't be necessary, Miss Sprite," he coldly replies, running his eyes over me once.

I grit my teeth. "It was a difficult mission. We

were underprepared for it, and none of the usual tactics for taking down a shifter worked. It went a little wrong from the start, and I do apologize for that."

"A little wrong," he slowly repeats my answer.

Here we go.

He stands up from his desk and walks over to his window. "Come with me."

I reluctantly follow him over, standing at his side as he towers over me. I hate being short at times. "A little wrong is when you make a small mistake that no one notices what you did and it doesn't attract attention. M.A.D. is known for discreetly dealing with supernaturals who have turned into monsters, for the queen. Destroying two buildings would suggest it went very wrong and quite the opposite of what your job stands for."

"Boss—"

"And furthermore, my boss is breathing down my neck to fire you. He is questioning why two of my junior associates have somehow managed to destroy two fucking expensive buildings. Explain it to me. Now, Miss Sprite."

"Technically, the monster destroyed the buildings when it had a tantrum and reacted badly to the enchanted wolfbane," I quietly answer.

"If you were struggling, you should have sent for help," he commands. "Not taken it on yourself with a new enforcer."

"We didn't have time, or it would have escaped and killed more mortals," I sharply reply. "Isn't that the real job? To save lives?"

An awkward silence drifts between us, and I steel my back for his reply. "You're meant to be instructing your partner on how to responsibly take on monsters. What you did today was teach her that you can take on a hybrid, alone, and somehow survive by the skin of your teeth. When she goes out and repeats your lesson alone, she will be hurt. Even die."

Guilt presses down on my chest. "But, boss—"

"Yes, Miss Sprite?" he interrupts, challenging me to say anything but *I'm sorry* with those cold grey eyes of his. When I first met Merrick Night, I thought he was the most beguiling mortal I'd ever met. Then he opened his perfectly shaped lips and made me want to punch him.

I look away first and over the city, the last bits of light dying away over the horizon. "There's been so many of these hybrid creatures recently, all over Wyvcelm. I have contacts in Junepit and Goldway City who told me as much. Where are they coming from? What caused them to be like that?"

"That is classified, Miss Sprite," he coolly replies. Basically, it's well above my pay grade to ask.

"It's probably not safe for everyone to go out in twos on missions like this anymore," I counter.

"Your only defense is that you secured the monster without Miss Mist using her voice," he says with a hint of cool amusement. "That would have been a real fuckup for us all to deal with."

Fuckup would be an understatement. The sirens' most deadly power, among many, is their enchanted voice when they sing the old language of the fae. Instantly, she would lure every male in the entire vicinity towards her, monster or not, and they would bow to her alone. Mortal females like me would be left screaming for the dragon goddess to save us, holding our hands over our ears, begging for death. Her voice stretches for at least two to three miles, and only a full-blooded fae can resist it. I've only heard it once, and personally, I never want to hear it again. I can still hear it now, like an old echo that draws me to her, a flash of the old power of the sirens who used to rule this world before the fae rose to power.

"Am I fired or can I leave, boss?"

He links his fingers, leaning back in the chair, which creaks. "I'm itching to dock your pay for this. But I won't. Not this time. You can go."

"Thank you," I say sarcastically and turn on my heel.

"Miss Sprite?" I stop mid-step and look back at him. "Don't make me regret being lenient on you today. You should know better."

I nod before turning away. "Fucking asshole," I whisper under my breath. He's not supernatural, and I know he can't hear me, and it's not like I can actually call him that to his face. Then I'd be fired for sure. Still, I'm sure I hear him chuckle under his breath.

I rush down the steps and say goodbye to Wendy before leaving the enforcement building and going to the Royal Bank on the other side of the market. I withdraw my day's pay, wincing that it's not nearly as much as I need, but a few hundred coins will sort everything out, and I'll work a double shift at the end of this week so I can eat for the rest of the week.

After making my way through the market and grabbing some dried meats, I head into the complex where my apartment is, listening to the old tower creak and groan in the wind. My apartment is four hundred and seven out of eight hundred flats in the entire building, and it is owned by the Fae Queen, like everything else. I'm lucky I got a place here, in a decent side of town, and it is everything I've worked towards for a very long time. I take the steps two at a time until I get to the hundred level. The corridor is littered with bikes, toys and plants, like every family level.

I knock twice on door one hundred and seven before opening it up with my key and heading inside.

"It's just me," I shout out as I feel how cold it is in here and flick on the magical heating. The weather is always changing so quickly. Some say it's the old gods anger that changes the weather from hot to cold all within a day. I'll pay that bill later, either way. "Louie?"

"Here," Louie shouts back, and I follow his shout to find him in the open-plan kitchen-living area, also where he has a small bed pushed up at the one side. The walls are cracked, the cream paper peeling off, but it's the same in most of the apartments. Louie is sitting on the bed, throwing an orange ball in the air and catching it over and over.

Louie catches the ball one more time before sitting up, brushing locks of his black hair out of his eyes.

"How was school?" I question, leaning against the wall.

"Boring and predictable. Mr. French told me I was too smart for the class and suggested I join the fae army. Again," he tells me, and my heart lurches for a second until I see him chuckle. "I'm not crazy. Obviously."

After the age of ten, any male or female can join the fae army and be trained to fight for the queen, but they have to take the serum. The serum is an enchanted concoction that turns any mortal into a full-blooded fae and forces a bond between whoever takes it and the queen. Meaning that no one who takes the serum can ever betray her. I once thought about joining the fae army myself when things were rough and I was starving, but I will never forget the other foster kids in the homes who died from the serum. Roughly ten percent survive. I will never let Louie take a risk like that. Not even for the riches and security and the promise of power that the Fae Queen offers up.

I'm lost in my thoughts. I don't even notice Louie climb off his bed and come over to me. His eyes are like molten silver, just like his father's were. "You look tired."

"Hello, good to see you, too. How's your mom today?"

"The same," he quietly says, walking past me and opening the door to her bedroom. His mom was once a foster mom of mine, and the only one alive. I look down at her in her bed, her thin body covered in an unnatural blue glow as she lightly hovers off the bedsheets. Five years ago, we were attacked by the monster who has hunted me my entire life. Five years ago, her mate jumped in front of her to save her life, they smashed through a wall, and she hit her head on the edge of a door. My foster dad was the only reason I became an enforcer—because he was one. The Enforcer Guild paid for this apartment and a magically protected sleep until she can be woken, not that we can afford to do that, and the Guild's sympathy only stretched so far.

This was my eleventh foster home, the very last one I went to before I turned sixteen and aged out. I remember coming here, fearful, and meeting Louie, who hugged me. I hadn't been hugged in years, and it shocked me. It was still one of the happiest days of my life.

I go over to her side, stroking her greying red

hair and sighing. I'd do anything to be able to afford to wake her up. For Louie. For me.

I leave three quarters of my wages on the side, and Louie looks down at the money, right as his stomach grumbles. I smile and nod. "Should I go and get something for us?" he asks.

"And for the week. For you," I tell him, ruffling his hair.

"Thank you," he says quietly. "One day, I'm going to be an enforcer like you and pay you back for all these years. I'm going to protect you."

"You're my brother in every way that matters, and family don't owe each other debts like this," I gently tell him. "And with how smart you are, I hope to the goddess you become someone so much better than me."

"Impossible," he says with a grin.

"Be careful on the streets," I warn him as he picks up a few of the coins and shoves them into his faded brown trousers. I need to buy him some new clothes soon, judging from the tears and holes in his blue shirt. One thing I love about Louie is that he never complains, never asks for clothes or for anything that costs money except for food. I wish I could give him more, but I can't.

"The monsters can't catch me, I'm too fast," he exclaims before bolting out of the door.

I chuckle as I sit down in the chair by the side of her bed, picking up her pale hand. "He doesn't have a clue, does he, mom? But he looks so much like dad."

Silence and the gentle hum of the magic surrounding her is my only reply, and I can't even remember what her voice is like anymore. She was my foster mom for a few years, far longer than any of the other ten before her, and she always asked me to call her *mom*. "One day, I'm going to wake you up so you can see Louie growing into a strong man. I'm going to make sure he gets a good job and stays far away from the true dangers of this city."

I hope she can hear me. I hope it gives her some comfort to know I'm here, but a part of me wonders if she would resent me. I'm the reason she is like this. I'm the reason her mate is dead. I close my eyes and blow out a shaky breath. The monster hasn't come back, not for years, and I have no reason to suspect he will now. But if he does, this time, I won't be a helpless child, unable to stop him from murdering my foster parents. I don't know if he killed my biological parents, no one does, but he killed every enforcer family that took me in. I try not to think of it, of all the death that haunted me like he did. My monster, my lurking shadow. I stay with my foster mom for a little longer before cleaning up the house, doing the washing and tidying in her room before Louie gets back, and then we cook dinner together before eating.

"Can I come to yours to play a game of kings?" he asks, referring to the card game we play on quiet nights, especially weekends like today, as I wash up and he dries the plates.

"I'd usually have you over, but I'm meeting Nerelyth for drinks tonight. It's her birthday," I tell him softly. Most kids his age would prefer to play with their friends and have them over, but Louie has never been good at making friends. He keeps to himself.

"Okay," he replies, his voice tinged with sadness. Loneliness. He only has me and his mom, but she can't read him stories, play games and help with the complicated enchantment work he is learning at school. After grabbing my bag, I kiss the top of his head before I leave, closing the door behind me and resting my head back against it, my eyes drooping. I'm so tired and I could use a long nap, not a night of partying for Nerelyth's birthday.

I sigh and push myself off the wall before

heading up to my apartment. It is partially paid for by the Enforcer Guild, one of the half decent things they do for their employees. The night sky glitters like a thousand moons as I get to my floor and look up at the sunroof far above. Three actual moons hang in the sky somewhere, but I can't see them from here, and I wish I could. They say looking at the three moons and making a wish is the only way for the dragon goddess to hear you. I'm sure it's not true, but I still look up sometimes and wish. I shove my key into the lock, wondering if I have any enchanted wine left over from last time Nerelyth came over, and push into my cold apartment. If I get dressed quickly, I might even have time to finish the extremely spicy romance book I was reading last night, on the way to the bar.

"Posy, where are you?" I shout out as I head in. "I bought some of those meat strips you like from the market, as I'm going out tonight with Nerelyth. It's her birthday, remember?"

I've been mostly absent for the last two days and not had much time to spend with Posy—my roommate who happens to be a bat and stuck that way thanks to a witch's curse. I drop my bag on the side and look around in the darkness before sighing. Clicking my fingers, balls of warm white light within small glass spheres flood my apartment with light from where they are attached to the wall. I search around the main area, a small kitchen with two counters, a magical food storage box, and a large worn sofa pressed against the wall. It looks nearly the same as when I moved in, I notice, except for my two bookcases in the corridor leading to the bathroom and bedroom, full of romance books I've collected over the years. My prized possessions.

Escapism at its finest.

"Posy, come on. You can't still be mad at me?" I holler in frustration as I walk into the tiny bathroom, which is empty. "Bats are nocturnal, so I know you're awake and ignoring me, but I don't have time to chase you around this apartment all night."

I hear a small rustling noise from my bedroom, and I smile as I walk over and push the door open.

Clicking my fingers, two lights burn to life above my bed, and I go still. My heart nearly stops because it's not Posy in my bedroom.

There's a monster sitting on my bed.

BONUS READ OF HEIR OF MONSTERS

*L*arge wings.

Grey skin.

Muscular, massive shoulders and thick arms.

"Get the hell out!" I shout, a scream dying in my throat as I take a step away. I pull my dagger out from the clip on my thigh and hold it out between us as I quickly look for Posy, not seeing her anywhere. There's a friggin' monster in my room.

A wave of magic whips into my hand, the sting of it cold and piercing. My dagger flips across the room as I flinch, and it embeds itself in the wall with a thud. The monster doesn't even lift its head. He's... reading—my spicy romance book, of all things—as he sits on my bed. My double bed looks tiny with him sitting there, his dark hair soft and curling down his shoulders.

What the fuck?

My eyes widen as I look at this monster. He's a male. That much I'm sure of, and he's huge. He's sitting in the middle of my bed, reading my book from last night, looking like he's meant to be there. His skin is dark grey and almost velvety. Massive black wings stretch out of his back, but they're pulled in at his sides. Black horns curl out of the top of his thick black hair on his head, and if he wasn't a monster, I might even say he's handsome. He's shirtless, and he has pants on, but a tiny weird part of me focuses on the lack of a shirt for a second. No one looks that good shirtless—except this monster, it seems.

He is so big, and I'm sure he could snap me like a twig. Who the hell is he? What is he? More importantly—why is he in my bedroom?

"This is an interesting book for an innocent doe like you to be reading, Calliophe Maryann Sprite."

I freeze, my heart pounding as his deep, sensual voice fills my room. How does he know my full name?

He looks up at me with hauntingly beautiful amethyst eyes and smirks. "Speechless, Doe?"

"Get the fuck out of my room!" I shout, grabbing the nearest thing on my side table and throwing it at him. He catches the stuffed purple teddy bear in his hand, then raises an eyebrow as his lips twitch with humor.

"Don't run," he purrs.

I glare as I grab the next thing, which is a cheap statue of the goddess, and I throw that straight at him instead. The statue crashes into his hand, smashes into pieces on impact, and he simply sighs in annoyance as he begins to stand. My old bed creaks as I grab my precious books from the corridor as I back away and throw them at him as I retreat. He catches them all like it's a game. I can't hear anything but my heartbeat, and I can't see anything but those wings that have haunted me for so many years. My monster had wings. It's all I can remember of him before he killed every parent I ever had.

Wings. The beat of wings fills my ears as I burn with anger. My monster is back to kill me. I turn and run to the sofa, jumping on it as I pull out the two daggers I have hidden down on one side and crouch down in the corner. He casually strolls down the corridor, and he blocks the way to the only exit from my apartment as he faces me and crosses his arms. "Do you really believe that you, a tiny little mortal, will be able to stop me?"

"Come closer. Find out," I taunt. If he is going to kill me, I'm going down with a fight. I haven't survived monsters all these years, my entire life, to die easily at the hands of one.

He laughs, the sound deep and frightening. Arrogant son of a bitc—

I see a flash of black right before Posy flies straight into his face, clawing at him with her tiny, almost purple, bat wings. Posy is only a tiny bat and no more than the size of his hand as he grabs her by the scruff of her neck and holds her up in front of him. She still fights. The more I look at him, I realize he can't be the monster who hunted me. Those purple eyes aren't black, dark and cold like my monster's were. Still, those wings... my monster must be what he is. "What is this thing?" he asks.

I would laugh if he wasn't trying to kill me. Posy yells, "Die, die, die. You supernatural monster! This is my home, and I don't care how horny my roommate is. She is not fucking a monster when I'm living here!"

By the old gods. My cheeks burn.

The monster smirks and looks over at me. "You have a talking bat."

"Let her go!" I demand as I look between them and the door. I don't know how I will make it to the door to run if I go for Posy.

He sighs, and Posy is still ranting away, unaware that no one is listening to her anymore. Or the fact this monster isn't my date and that he is here to kill me. "No. We are leaving."

"We are not," I say at the same time Posy declares, "Finally. Go to the monster's place and do the dirty. Between keeping me here as your pet and your new fuck buddy, I think you have a weird thing for bats."

"We bats can be very fun," the monster agrees with a hint of dry amusement that makes him seem almost mortal. Almost. He is very much not.

He lets Posy go, and she flies into my bedroom, slamming the door shut. I need a better roommate/pet. Posy sucks.

"Then go and have fun somewhere else, or I'm going to pin those nice wings of yours to my wall," I say, holding the daggers up higher. Why he hasn't used his magic to rid me of them yet floats into the back of my mind. Maybe he is playing with me. "What are you, anyway?"

"Wyern," he coolly answers. "Haven't you seen any in your career?"

No, I haven't, or I'd be very dead. My blood runs cold as I take him in, a Wyern male, in my living room. The Wyerns are immortal, deadly, and everyone knows they are forbidden from entering Ethereal City. Some say they are fae—an old race of them. Some say they were created by the fae and are born monsters.

I should have known he's not a monster. Not exactly, but not far from one. From what I know, the Wyerns live in the Forgotten Lands, a punishment from my queen for the war they started thousands of years ago. Some say the sirens siding with the Fae Queen was the only way we won.

One trained Wyern male can slaughter ten trained fae in minutes.

My heart races as I take all of this in. If I call for help and they find me here with him, even if he is trying to kill me or take me somewhere, the queen will execute me for treason. "If the queen finds you here, which she will, we are both dead. Leave."

He steps towards me, an amused smirk on his lips. "Your precious queen would be very honored if I turned up in her city, but perhaps a little angry I came for you and not to see her."

"What?"

He glowers at me. "Are you mortals truly this dense? We. Are. Leaving."

"We certainly are not going anywhere!"

He takes another step forward, and I start to back away until the back of my knees touch the sofa.

I lash out at him with my daggers, cutting through his arm, and it bubbles with blood. He doesn't even notice as he grabs my hands, squeezing tight enough I'm forced to drop the daggers with a yelp. I kick at his shin, which is like a rock and only hurts me, and he grabs me by the waist and throws me over his shoulder like I weigh nothing. I scream and kick him in the stomach and slam my hands on his solid back, but nothing makes his arm shift from his iron tight grip on me.

Magic wraps around me firmly, its icy sting burning into my skin, and I hiss in pain as my head spins. I hate magic.

"Let me go!" I scream over and over. He only laughs like it's deeply amusing to him as he walks out of my apartment by kicking my front door open. I look up in horror as he spreads his massive wings out, and magic lashes around us as he shoots up the flights of stairs. The stairs whip up around us as I scream, ducking my head as my stomach feels like a million butterflies have burst to life. He crashes through the glass, bits of it cutting into my arms, and launches us into the night sky above the city. His wings beat near my face, and I stop trying to fight him. If he drops me, I'm dead.

It doesn't stop the lash of magic that slams into my head and knocks me out cold seconds later, leaving me dreaming of wings and star-filled night skies.

THE MISSING WOLF

LEAVING THE PAST BEHIND.

ANASTASIA

I stand still on the side of the train tracks, letting the cold wind blow my blonde and purple dip-dyed hair across my face. I squeeze the handle of my suitcase tighter, hoping that the train will come soon. *It's freezing today, and my coat is packed away in the suitcase, dammit.* I feel like I've waited for this day for years, the day I get to leave my foster home and join my sister at college. I look behind me into the parking lot, seeing my younger sister stood watching me go, my foster grandmother holding her hand. Phoebe is only eleven years old, but she is acting strong today, no matter how much she wants me to stay. I smile at her, trying to ignore how difficult it feels to leave her here, but I know she couldn't be in a better home. I can get through college with our older sister and then get a job in the city, while living all together. *That's the plan anyway.*

We lost our mum and dad in a car accident ten years ago, and we were more than lucky to find a foster parent that would take all three of us in. Grandma Pops is a special kind of lady. She is kind and loves to cook, and the money she gets from fostering pays for her house. She lost her two children in a fire years ago, and she tells us regularly that we keep her happy and alive. Even if we do eat a lot for three kids. Luckily, she likes to look after us as I burn everything I attempt to cook. And I don't even want to remember the time I tried to wash my clothes, which ended in disaster.

"Train four-one-nine to Liverpool is calling at the station in one minute," the man announces over the loudspeaker, just before I hear the sound of the train coming in from a distance. I turn back to see the grey train speeding towards us, only slowing down when it gets close, but I still have to walk to get to the end carriage. I wait for the two men in front of me to get on before I step onto the carriage, turning to pull my suitcase on. I search through the full seats until I find an empty one near the back, next to a window. I have to make sure it's facing the way the train is going as it freaks me out to sit the other way. I slide my suitcase under the seat before sitting down, leaving my handbag on the small table in front of me.

I wave goodbye to my sister, who waves back, her head hidden on grandma's shoulder as she cries. I can only see her waist length, wavy blonde hair before the train pulls away. I'm going to miss her. *Urgh, it's not like we don't have phones and FaceTime!* I'm being silly. I pull my phone out of my bag and quickly send a message to my older sis, letting her know I am on the train. I also send a message to Phoebe, telling her how much I love and miss her already.

"Ticket?" the train employee guy asks, making me jump out of my skin, and my phone falls on the floor.

"Sorry! I'm always dropping stuff," I say, and the man just stares at me with a serious expression, still holding his hand out. His uniform is crisply ironed, and his hair is combed to the left without a single hair out of place. I roll my eyes and pull my bag open, pulling out my ticket and handing it to him. After he checks it for about a minute, he scribbles on it before handing it back to me. I've never understood why they bother drawing on the tickets when the machines check the tickets at the other end anyway. I put my ticket back into my bag before sliding it under the seat just as the train moves, jolting me a little.

I reach for my phone, which is stuck to some paper underneath it. I've always been taught to pick up rubbish, so I grab the paper as well as my phone before slipping out from under the table and back to my seat. I put my phone back into my handbag before looking at the leaflet I've picked up. It's one of those warning leaflets about familiars and how it is illegal to hide one. The leaflet has a giant lion symbol at the top and warning signs around the edges. It explains that you have to call the police and report them if you find one.

Familiars account for 0.003 percent of the human race, though many say they are nothing like humans and don't like to count them as such. Familiars randomly started appearing about fifty years ago, or at least publicly they did. A lot of people believe they just kept themselves hidden before that. The Familiar Empire was soon set up, and it is the only place safe for familiars to live in peace. They have their own laws, an alliance with humans, and their own land in Scotland, Spain and North America.

Unfortunately, anyone could suddenly become a familiar, and you wouldn't know until one random day. It can be anything from a car crash to simply waking up that sets off the gene, but once a familiar, always a familiar. They have the mark on their hand, a glowing tattoo of whatever animal is bonded to them. The animals are the main reason familiars are so dangerous. They have a bond with one animal who would do anything for them. Even kill. And I heard once that some kid's animal was a lion as big as an elephant. But those are just the things we know publicly, who knows what is hidden behind the giant walls of the Familiar Empire?

"My uncle is one, you know?" a girl says, and I look up to see a young girl about ten years old hanging over her seat, her head tilted to the side as she stares at the leaflet in my hand. "He has a big rabbit for a familiar."

"That's awesome..." I say, smiling as I put the leaflet down. I bet picking up giant rabbit poo isn't that awesome, but I don't tell her that.

"I want to be a familiar when I grow up," she excitedly says. "They have cool powers and pets! Mum won't even let me get a dog!"

"Sit down, Clara! Stop talking to strangers!" her mum says, tugging the girl's arm, and she sits down after flashing me a cheeky grin.

I fold the leaflet and slide it into my bag before resting back in the seat, watching the city flash by from the window. I couldn't think of anything worse than being a familiar. You have to leave your family, your whole life, and live in the woods. *Being a familiar seems like nothing but a curse.*

THE MISSING WOLF

WHO WEARS A CLOAK THESE DAYS?

"Ana!!" my sister practically screeches as I step off the train, and then throws herself at me before I get a second to really look at her. Even though my sister is only a few inches taller than my five-foot-four self, she nearly knocks me over. I pull her blonde hair away from my face as it tries to suffocate me before she thankfully pulls away. I'm not a hugger, but Bethany always ignores that little fact.

"I missed you too, Bethany," I mutter, and she grins at me. Bethany was always the beautiful sister, and as we got older, she just got prettier. Seems the year at college has only added to that. Her blonde hair is almost white, falling in perfect waves down her back. Mine is the same, but I dyed the ends a deep purple. Another one of my attempts at sticking out in a crowd when I usually become invisible next to my gorgeous sister. Phoebe is the image of Bethany, and both of them look like photos of our mother. Whereas I look like my dad mostly, I still have the blonde hair. Bethany grins at me, then slowly runs her eyes over my outfit before letting out a long sigh.

"You look so pretty, sis," she says, and I roll my eyes. Bethany hates jeans and long-sleeved tops, which I happen to be wearing both. I didn't even look at what I threw on this morning. I shiver as the cold wind blows around me, reminding me that I should have gotten my coat out my suitcase on the train trip. It is autumn.

"You're such a bad liar," I reply, arching an eyebrow at her, and she laughs.

"Well, you are eighteen now, and I've never seen you in a dress. College is going to change all that." She waves a hand like she has sorted all the problems out.

"How so? I'm not wearing a dress to classes," I say, frowning at her. "Leggings are much easier to run around in, I think."

"Parties, of course," she tuts, laughing like it should be obvious. Bethany grabs hold of my suitcase before walking down the now empty sidewalk to the parking lot at the end.

"I need to study. There is no way I'm going to ace my nursing classes without a lot of studying," I tell her. Bethany took drama, and I wasn't the least bit surprised when she was offered a job at the end of her course, depending on her grades. Though she was an A-star student throughout high school, so there is no way she could fail.

"I love that you will have the same job mum

did," she eventually tells me, and I glance over at her as she smiles sadly at me before focusing back on where she is walking. I remember my mum and dad, whereas Bethany is just over one year older than me and remembers a lot more. Phoebe doesn't remember them at all; she only has our photos and the things we can tell her. It was difficult for Bethany to leave us both to come to college, but grandma and I told her she had to find a future.

"I doubt I will do it as well as her...but I like to help people. I know this is the right thing for me to do," I reply, and I see her nod in the corner of my eye. I quickly walk forward and hold the metal gate to the car park open for Bethany to walk through before catching up with her as we walk past cars.

"You've always been the nice one. I remember when you were twelve, and the boy down the road broke up with you because some other girl asked him out. The next day, that boy fell off his bike, cutting all his leg just outside our home. You helped him into the house, put plasters on his leg, and then walked his bike back to his house for him," she remarks. "Most people wouldn't have done that. I would have just laughed at him before leaving him on the sidewalk."

"I also called him a dumbass," I say, laughing at

the memory of his shocked face. "So I wasn't all that nice."

"That's why you are so amazing, sis," she laughs, and I chuckle as we get to Bethany's car. It's a run down, black Ford Fiesta, but I know Bethany adores the old thing. Even if there are scratches and bumps all over the poor car from Bethany's terrible driving.

"Get in, I can put the suitcase in the boot," she says, and I pull the passenger door open before sliding inside. I do my seatbelt up before resting back, watching out of the passenger window at the train pulling out of the station. There is a man in a black cloak stood still in the middle of the path, the wind pushing his cloak around his legs, but his hood is up, covering his face. I just stare, feeling stranger and more freaked out by the second as the man lifts his head. I see a flash of yellow under his hood for a brief moment, and I sit forward, trying to see more of the strange man I can't pull my eyes from. I almost jump out of my skin when Bethany gets in the car, slamming her door shut behind her, and I look over at her.

"Are you okay? You look pale," she asks, reaching over to put her hand on my head to check my temperature before pulling it away. I look back towards the man, seeing that he and the train are gone. Everything is quiet, still and creepy. *Time to go.*

"Yeah, everything is fine. I'm just nervous about my first day," I tell her, which is sort of honest, but I'm missing the little fact about the weird hooded man. *I mean, who walks around in cloaks like friggin' Darth Vader?* She frowns at me, seeing through my lies easily, but after I don't say a word for a while, she drops it.

"It will be fine. Don't worry!" she says, reaching over to squeeze my hand before starting the car. I keep my eyes on the spot the man was in until I can't see it anymore. I close my eyes and shake my head, knowing it was just a creepy guy, and I need to forget it. This is my first day of my new life, and nothing is going to ruin that.

Printed in Great Britain
by Amazon